THE ROYAL BALLET SCHOOL

Diaries

1

Ellie's Chance to Dance

Written by Alexandra Moss

Grosset & Dunlap • New York

For the students of The Royal Ballet School—
past, present, and future.
May you live your dreams—A.M.

Special thanks to
Veronica Bennett and Sue Mongredien

Series created by Working Partners Ltd

Copyright © 2005 by Working Partners Ltd. All rights reserved. Published by Grosset & Dunlap, a division of Penguin Young Readers Group, 345 Hudson Street, New York, New York 10014. GROSSET & DUNLAP is a trademark of Penguin Group (USA) Inc. Printed in the U.S.A.

Library of Congress Cataloging-in-Publication Data

Moss, Alexandra.
   Ellie's chance to dance / written by Alexandra Moss.
      p. cm. — (The Royal Ballet School diaries ; #1)
   Summary: After moving from Chicago to Oxford, England, ten-year-old Ellie worries about making new friends at school and caring for her mother who has multiple sclerosis, while also preparing to audition for the resident dancers training program at London's Royal Ballet School.
   ISBN 0-448-43535-7 (pbk.)
   [1. Ballet dancing—Fiction. 2. Moving, Household—Fiction. 3. Mothers and daughters—Fiction. 4. Interpersonal relations—Fiction. 5. Multiple sclerosis—Fiction. 6. Royal Ballet. School—Fiction. 7. Oxford (England)—Fiction. 8. England—Fiction.] I. Title.
   PZ7.M8515El 2005
   [Fic]—dc22

                                        2004013156

ISBN 0-448-43535-7   10 9 8 7 6 5 4 3

Chapter 1

Dear Diary,

This is it. So long, Chicago. England, here I come! I'm writing this on the plane somewhere over the Atlantic. I can't BELIEVE we've left America. I can't BELIEVE I just said good-bye to Grandma and Gramps at the airport, and to Heather, my best friend in the world. What am I gonna do without her?

It was horrible saying good-bye. I could hardly talk, my throat felt so tight. Heather gave me this journal, so I can write down everything that happens in Oxford. She said it would be almost the same as talking to her. I wish!

It's a good time to start a journal though, because my whole life is changing. It's a pretty weird feeling. I'm kind of excited and scared and freaked out, all at once.

We're leaving Chicago, the city where I grew up, to live in Oxford, England. Things are going great for Mom now. She's got her dream job as a professor at Oxford University—and she hasn't had an MS attack for ages. It must be so scary having multiple sclerosis. It affects her nerves—sometimes she gets trembly and drops things. Anyway, fingers crossed the MS attacks will stay away for a while longer. Sometimes I can almost forget that she has it.

She's been thrilled about the move to England, but I've gotta say, at first, I was totally unthrilled about it. I mean, I was all set to apply for the Joffrey Ballet School in Chicago, along with a couple of other girls in Ms. Lane's ballet class. But when she found out about the move to England, Ms. Lane said maybe I could apply to go to The Royal Ballet School instead. She is such a cool teacher. I am really going to miss her!

Anyway, Mom and I looked up The Royal Ballet School on the Internet—and that changed everything! The Royal Ballet School is one of the best places in the WORLD to study ballet. So many amazing dancers have trained there—Darcey Bussell, Dame Margot Fonteyn, Dame Antoinette Sibley . . .

You have to be eleven to go to The Royal Ballet School full-time, and I'm only ten—but they have this program for younger kids called Junior Associates. They hold classes every other Saturday in cities around England—including classes at The Royal Ballet School itself, right in the center of London. When Mom said London wasn't so very far away from Oxford, and how about applying, I was like, okay, I'll go to England right now, Mom!

I was kind of joking, but she helped me fill out the application—and soon after that, I received an invitation to audition!

The audition was back in June, and Mom and I flew over to London especially for it. It was really exciting coming to London just for me. Nerve-racking too, though. And I got in! Me, Ellie Brown, at The Royal Ballet School! You'd better believe it.

That was three months ago. And now we're moving to a different country, I'm starting Junior Associate classes, not to mention a new school, and I'm also starting

weekly classes at a local ballet school in
Oxford . . .

   I mean, could there be any more new
things in my life? I don't think so! Talk
about pressure—it's going to be one new
start after another. I just hope I can do
everything okay.

   Anyway, whatever happens, hopefully
Heather will be right, and there'll be lots of
exciting stuff to write down in this journal.
Watch this space!

How people ever managed to fall asleep on airplanes was
beyond Ellie. She was always far too excited to miss a second! Yet
her mom had snoozed practically the entire way from Chicago to
London, and now that they were on a train heading for Oxford,
she seemed to be dozing off all over again!

Ellie hadn't slept at all. They'd taken a night flight from
Chicago, which left at eight in the evening and landed at
Heathrow Airport seven hours later. So even though her watch
said ten-thirty British time, it was really . . .

She rubbed her gritty eyes, trying to work it out. Ahh. No
wonder she was feeling a little spacey. According to Chicago
time, it was five-thirty in the morning. Ouch! Not a good time
to be awake!

Ellie gazed out of the train window, watching the green fields and small towns rush by, smiling to herself as she listened to the family across the aisle. There was a mom and dad and two little kids who kept giggling to each other. It tickled Ellie every time they said anything. She just couldn't get used to hearing everybody talking with an English accent.

Ellie and her mom were traveling light, with just a couple of suitcases and a bag each to carry. All the rest of their stuff had been boxed up and was being shipped over to their new apartment in Oxford. Ellie thought about how strange their things were going to look in a new home. The wooden clock that had stood for as long as she could remember on their Chicago mantelpiece, for example—she just couldn't imagine it sitting anyplace else. And the thought of her ballet shoes and leotards going into a new closet—in a new bedroom—that was too freaky for words.

Ellie stiffened in excitement as the train began to slow.

"The train is now approaching Oxford station," came a voice over the loudspeaker. Oxford! They were here!

"Mom, Mom, wake up," Ellie said, patting her mom's arm. "This is us!"

The train pulled into the platform, and Ellie and her mom stepped out. Oxford station was kind of dull-looking with its long platforms and modern, brightly lit ticket office and sandwich bars. Ellie couldn't help feeling a knot of disappointment in her stomach. "I thought Oxford was supposed to be pretty?" she said to her mom as they heaved their suitcases onto a luggage trolley.

Her mom yawned and smiled at her. "Don't you worry, honey," she said. "The city itself is way more beautiful than the train station, trust me!"

Ellie and her mom waited in line for a taxi. Then, once they were inside the car, Mrs. Brown leaned forward to speak to the driver. "This is my daughter's first time in Oxford," she told him. "Would you mind driving past a few of the sights on the way to Tenniel College, please?"

The driver turned and winked at Ellie. "Brilliant," he said. "One grand tour of Oxford coming right up!"

"Thank you," Ellie said, excited at the thought of seeing her new home. Her mom had studied here years ago and had fallen in love with the city. As long as Ellie could remember, her mom had dreamed of coming back to live here. She hadn't been able to resist applying for the job of professor at the university when she'd seen it advertised. "It's fate," she'd said with a delighted look on her face. "It's definitely fate, Ellie!"

As the taxi driver drove them into the center of Oxford, Ellie's eyes widened. The streets were packed with the most amazing old sandstone college buildings, all crammed in next to one another, with small leaded windows, ornate carvings, and bell towers that jostled for position with the spires of the churches and the cathedral. The driver pointed out the Botanic Gardens and the picturesque Christ Church Meadow with its lush green slopes. It was the end of summer, and the leaves on the trees were turning fiery red, orange, and russet brown.

Ellie was dazzled. "I can't believe we're going to be living here, Mom," she breathed. "It's like something out of a movie."

Mrs. Brown nodded. "Just wait until you see our apartment," she said, her eyes shining.

As a professor at the university, Mrs. Brown was eligible for a staff apartment in a college building. Ellie hadn't been too thrilled at the thought of that, back in Chicago. She was used to her comfortable house in the suburbs, with its big backyard.

The taxi pulled up outside an ancient honey-colored stone block with huge, black double doors and arched, leaded windows. The building was so utterly charming, Ellie instantly changed her mind. "Wow," she gulped. "Wait till I tell Heather about this!"

After Mrs. Brown had paid the driver, they picked up keys from the porter's lodge and started to heave their heavy suitcases up the stairs of the building. Ellie was just starting to wish they could have had an apartment on the ground floor when a friendly-looking man appeared behind them, smiling.

"Can I help you with those?" he asked. He stuck out a hand. "Peter Minton. Lecturer in genetics."

Smiling her thanks, Mrs. Brown shook his hand. "Hello. Nice to meet you," she said. "I'm Amy Brown and this is my daughter, Ellie. We're moving onto the first floor."

"Ah, then we'll be neighbors," Mr. Minton said. He turned to Ellie. "Pleased to meet you, Ellie. My daughter Phoebe is around your age. She'll be delighted you're moving in." He picked up the cases. "You must be in number 4, across the hallway from us. Our old neighbors moved out last month. Once you've settled in, you must both come round for a cup of tea."

"That's very kind. We'd love to," Mrs. Brown smiled as they reached their front door. "Ah, there we are," she said. "Number 4."

When Mr. Minton had gone, Ellie rushed around the apartment looking at everything. It was small compared to their old home in Chicago, but it was light and bright, with great views of the beautiful college gardens from the windows.

There were two bedrooms—one with a double bed, one with a single. Ellie sat down on the single bed and bounced on it a few times. She pulled her battered, little teddy bear from her bag. "Welcome to your new home," she told him. "*Our* new home. What do you think?" She hugged him close to her and breathed in his familiar smell. Suddenly, she missed Chicago an awful lot. "No, I'm not too sure either," she told him. "Pretty weird, isn't it? I wonder how long it'll take before it *feels* like home."

Her mom poked her head around the door. "I'm going to freshen up and brush my teeth," she said. "Then let's go meet our new neighbors."

"Sure," Ellie replied. She looked down at her watch. "Wow, everyone at home is only just getting up now, Mom," she said. "Grandma and Gramps will be making coffee and breakfast. Weird, isn't it?"

Mrs. Brown patted her stomach. "The thought's making me

hungry," she said. "We'll say hello to the Mintons and then go out to eat. Would you like to try fish-and-chips for lunch? When I used to live here, it was my favorite English food. It's fish fried in batter, served with french fries and vinegar. You'll love it."

Ellie's mom had spent a semester at Oxford when she was an art student. That was how she'd met Ellie's dad. Ellie wished she could remember her dad better—he'd died in a car accident when she was very young, just a baby, practically. Ever since then, it had been Ellie and her mom, a close-knit unit. And even though vinegar and french fries sounded pretty weird to Ellie, she trusted her mom and guessed it was worth a shot. She had promised her mom she'd keep a positive attitude about the move—and that included English cuisine!

She gave her mom a smile. "Fish-and-chips sounds great to me."

•   •   •   •

Phoebe Minton had the blondest hair and the biggest smile Ellie had ever seen. She wasn't at all shy, either. Almost as soon as Ellie and her mom had entered the Mintons' apartment, Phoebe pulled Ellie away to her bedroom so they could talk in private.

"So you'll be going to Tenniel Junior School, like me?" Phoebe asked, once they were in her room. "Fab! We can walk there together. Term starts on Monday, did you know? Only three days left of the holiday." She groaned dramatically and flopped back on her bed.

"What's school like?" Ellie wanted to know.

Phoebe sat up again. "Don't worry, everyone's really nice," she smiled. "We've got Miss Welch as our teacher this year. She is soooo cool. She took us for a few weeks last term when Mr. Fields, our usual teacher, was ill. Do you like art? She's really big on art. Personally, I am the worst artist in the world, but even I made things that looked okay with Miss Welch."

Talking with Phoebe was like trying to keep up in a race, Ellie soon realized. English accents were cool and all—but they were hard to understand!

By the time Ellie's mom came tapping on the door, saying it was time to go, Ellie knew that it was going to be fun having Phoebe as a friend. Even better, she only had to cross the hallway to see her!

"Come over at the weekend if you want a *proper* tour of Oxford," Phoebe said. "We can walk along the river and take a picnic if it's sunny. Or we can hire a rowing boat and—"

"Phoebe, Phoebe," Mrs. Minton said, holding up her hands. "Just give Ellie a bit of space for a couple of days. The poor girl has only just got here, and she'll most probably have jet lag!"

"That's okay," Ellie said, smiling. But as they left the Mintons' apartment, a wave of tiredness rolled through her.

"Come on," her mom said, seeing her pale face. "You need food and then rest. Let's get something quickly. Diana Minton said there was a chip shop on the main street."

. . . . .

Ten minutes later, Ellie and her mom were walking back

through the college gardens clutching warm paper parcels of fish-and-chips. The parcels smelled wonderful, and Ellie couldn't resist unwrapping a corner to pull out a chip. It was thick, salty, golden, and chewy—not thin and crispy like American fries. She bit down, and the tang of vinegar exploded on her tongue. It was delicious!

"What do you think?" her mom asked.

Ellie swallowed her chip and pulled out another one. "I think English chips are my new favorite food," she said with a grin.

Chapter 2

"Ellie! Are you awake in there? Time to get up for school!"

Ellie blinked and looked around her new bedroom. She still wasn't used to waking up in this bed. Sure, it was the same quilt cover and pillow, and there were all her things around her, but it surprised her every time. *Oh, yeah. We moved. We're in Oxford.* She sat up and rubbed her eyes. *And school starts today!*

Ellie got out of bed, her tummy jumping with nerves. She hoped the other students would be as friendly as Phoebe. And she hoped she wouldn't do anything dumb on her first day!

After a hot shower, Ellie pulled on the strange new school uniform they'd bought on Saturday—a white blouse, gray skirt, and navy blue V-neck sweater.

"You look great, honey," her mom said fondly when she came into the kitchen for breakfast. "Try not to look so nervous—I'm sure you'll be fine."

Ten minutes later, there was a knock at the door.

It was Phoebe. "I thought we could walk to school together," she beamed. "Are you ready?"

Ellie smiled back as best she could. She was grateful that Phoebe was so thoughtful and friendly. "I think so," she said. "Bye, Mom."

"Bye, sweetheart," Mrs. Brown said, kissing Ellie's forehead. "Have a good day."

Phoebe and Ellie clattered down the apartment steps, then tramped across Tenniel College's neatly mown lawns and out to the street, toward Tenniel Junior School.

Phoebe gave Ellie a full briefing of what to expect, earnestly describing everyone in the class Ellie was joining. ". . . So don't listen to Jack Barton, he's a jerk, and so is Ben Davies . . ."

Ellie couldn't concentrate. She'd forgotten half the names already. She was dreading not knowing anybody, except for Phoebe. She stuffed her hands deep into her coat pockets. *In seven hours, I'll be back at the apartment,* she thought, trying to comfort herself, *and my first day will be over.*

"Well, this is it," Phoebe said as they walked through the school gates. She rolled her eyes comically. "Your new prison."

Ellie looked around. There was a large playground in front of them with crowds of kids yelling and charging around. Boys were kicking a soccer ball, some girls were jumping rope, and a bunch of younger kids were playing tag. At the far side of the playground was the school itself, a large red-brick building with old-fashioned chimneys at each end of the roof.

Ellie licked her lips nervously. All of a sudden, she wanted to be back at Rosemont Public School in good old

Chicago, with Heather and Libby and the rest of her old friends. But instead . . .

Phoebe was already running across the playground toward a group of girls, waving and shouting. "Hi, Maddie! How was Spain? Hi, Ruby! Hello, Tasha! Come and meet Ellie, everyone. She's my new neighbor and guess what—she's a *ballerina*!"

Ellie ran to catch up with Phoebe, feeling flustered at being stared at by so many people at once.

"Hello, I'm Maddie," said a friendly-faced girl with short, brown hair and bright blue eyes. "Wow—a ballerina! Is that true? Or is Pheebs talking rubbish, as usual?"

"I wouldn't exactly say I'm a ballerina," Ellie said. "I just take ballet classes, that's all."

"Hi, I'm Tasha," a petite, dark-haired girl said. "My sister Zoe's really into ballet, too. She takes classes at Franklin's on the other side of town."

"Oh!" Ellie blinked at the familiar-sounding name. At last— something she knew about! "I'm going there too. I have my first class there on Wednesday!"

"I'll tell her to look out for you," Tasha promised.

Phoebe introduced the others. "This is Lucy," she said, pointing to the girl with a funky blonde cropped hairstyle, wearing a bright pink jacket. "And this is Ruby," she went on. Ruby had a sweet, round face and shoulder-length blonde curls.

The tall, elegant dark-haired girl Phoebe introduced as Rachel was the only person who didn't smile back. In fact, Ellie thought

Rachel seemed to be gazing at her pretty coldly. Why was she looking at her that way?

"Hi," Ellie said. Her mouth suddenly felt so dry, the word came out as a croak.

"We'll test you on who's who later," said Ruby with a grin. "Just to be sure you were paying attention! I like your bag, by the way. Where did you get it?"

Ellie, feeling Rachel's cool stare upon her, found herself babbling. "A store in Chicago—that's where I'm from. We just moved here."

"My mum will be sooo excited," the girl called Lucy put in. "She's American, too—you wait, she'll be wanting updates on everything trendy back home."

"Cool. Mom will love that," Ellie said, smiling back at Lucy. "We—"

"Come on, everyone," Rachel said loudly, interrupting Ellie before she could finish her sentence. "Holly's here. Let's go and see if her mum said yes to the sleepover."

Ellie shut her mouth abruptly as the girls all followed Rachel over to a red-haired girl who was just coming through the school gates. Ellie trailed after them uncertainly. It was going to take her a while to settle in, that much was clear. She couldn't help thinking about her old gang of friends and all the sleepovers they'd had together. How long would it be before she was invited to a sleepover here?

A teacher blew a whistle, and then the whole school began to file into their classrooms.

"This way," Phoebe said, reappearing at Ellie's side. "Through this door and left."

Ellie was happy to have Phoebe as she followed her into the school building. Phoebe showed her where to hang her coat, and then they walked along a corridor and into a sunny classroom filled with tables and chairs.

A woman with short, dark hair and friendly brown eyes was sitting behind a desk. "Welcome, everybody," she said, getting to her feet. "As most of you already know, I'm Miss Welch, your teacher for this year. Let's hope we all get on wonderfully together—I'm sure we will!"

Ellie felt her heart thudding as she and the other students scraped chairs back to sit down. *Oh, I hope so*, she thought anxiously, catching sight of Rachel. *I really hope so!*

•   •   •   •

Ellie found the first few days at her new school quite hard. It wasn't having a new teacher or having new work to do. As Phoebe had said, Miss Welch was great—so that was okay. And the schoolwork didn't seem too different from what she'd studied back home in Chicago, either. Miss Welch had announced that they were going to be learning about kings and queens of England, which Ellie liked the sound of, and the class book they'd started reading was a very funny story about a junior magician. So that was all good, too. What *was* hard was feeling like a fish out of water.

As an American, Ellie felt so different from all the English girls. It wasn't so much the accent—it was getting used to all the funny phrases everyone used. She was learning a whole new vocabulary—it was like a different language! And they all seemed to think Ellie's phrases were weird, too! Every time she used the word "pants," the English girls collapsed into giggles.

"'Pants' doesn't mean 'trousers' over here," Phoebe explained. "It means knickers—you know, underwear!"

The worst thing was that while some of the girls were friendly toward Ellie—Phoebe, of course, and Ruby and Tasha, too—for some reason, the tall girl, Rachel, seemed to have taken an instant dislike to her. Rachel hadn't actually said anything to Ellie's face, but Ellie overheard her making sarcastic jokes about "our little ballerina" or "Madame Tippitoes." It made Ellie feel like an idiot every time. After all, it wasn't like she'd bragged about being a good dancer. She'd barely even mentioned it, but Rachel seemed to want to make a big deal out of it.

Ellie could see that Rachel was funny and popular, but she had a sharp tongue, and Ellie could tell that nobody wanted to challenge her, for fear of being teased. Ellie tried to ignore the name-calling, but it was hard. And, boy, did it make her miss Heather and her old friends.

. . . . .

It wasn't until Wednesday and her first lesson at the Franklin Dance Academy that Ellie felt herself relax. She just couldn't wait to pull on her leotard and ballet shoes again! Practicing at home just wasn't the same.

Ballet had been Ellie's passion since she was three years old—and it had become her escape, too. Whenever she danced, she forgot about everything—just focused on her body and the beauty of the classical ballet steps. With the upheaval of the move, Ellie had really missed the discipline of regular classes.

"Another new start," her mom said, hugging her good-bye at the entrance to the Franklin Dance Academy. "You've had so many new things happening to you this week, haven't you?"

Ellie nodded, feeling her feet tingle with happy anticipation at the very sight of the studio floor. From where she was standing, she could see a long barre in front of huge wall mirrors. She had really missed all of this! It felt like coming home. She had a pang of nostalgia as she thought about Ms. Lane, her old teacher, who'd taught Ellie from the start. Ms. Lane, who'd hugged Ellie so tightly when she'd said good-bye. "What am I going to do without my star pupil?" she'd sighed. "Make me proud, Ellie. Show those dancers in England what you can do!"

Ellie kissed her mom. "This new start is definitely gonna be a good one," she told her. "I can't wait!"

Ellie made her way to the changing room with the other students and put on the new black leotard and pink sweatshirt that made up the Franklin Academy uniform, plus a pair of white socks and her beloved ballet shoes. She tied her hair up and pinned it carefully into place, then went into the dance studio.

Ellie felt self-conscious as she walked in. The other students all seemed to be chatting and giggling in clusters, checking their hair in the mirrors together or concentrating on their warm-up stretches. There were about twenty in the class, mostly girls around Ellie's age, and a couple of boys, too. Ellie took a place at the barre near the back of the room and glanced around, wondering which girl was Tasha's sister Zoe. Maybe the girl with the jet-black bun and big blue eyes like Tasha's?

Ellie took a deep breath, about to go over and say hi, when a tall woman came into the studio. Mrs. Franklin, Ellie guessed, gazing at her curiously. She looked older than Ms. Lane, her teacher back in Chicago. Mrs. Franklin had gray hair and kind brown eyes. From her straight back and the way she held her head, anyone could tell she had trained as a dancer.

Mrs. Franklin looked straight at her, then came over to where she was standing. "Ellie Brown?"

Ellie nodded. "Hello," she said, feeling a little shy all of a sudden.

"Welcome, my dear," Mrs. Franklin said, patting her arm. "Very nice to see you. I'm sure you'll feel quite at home in this class, but if there's anything you're not sure of, just give me a shout."

"Thank you," Ellie said politely.

Mrs. Franklin went up to the front of the class and clapped her hands. "Hello," she said. "I hope you're feeling flexible today! Now then, we have a new member of class," she announced. "Step forward, Ellie. Everyone, this is Ellie Brown. She has just moved to Britain from the United States, so let's all make her feel welcome."

"Hi, Ellie!" one girl called out at once. She had brown hair pulled back in a bun with a silver ribbon wound around it, dimpled cheeks, and the most impish grin Ellie had ever seen.

Ellie smiled back at her, relieved to see such a friendly face. A couple of other girls were looking over at her in a friendly way, too, although most people were staring curiously. Ellie knew they'd all be wondering how good a dancer she'd be. She remembered feeling the same curiosity whenever new students had started in Ms. Lane's class. *I'll show them I can dance*, she thought, flexing her feet. *And I WILL make Ms. Lane proud!*

"Yes, thank you, Bethany," Mrs. Franklin said to the girl who'd called out hi. "Now, let's get started—*pliés* first. Positions at the barre, please, everyone."

Ellie went over to the barre with the rest of the class and turned her toes out to the side, in first position. She felt her muscles lengthen into a stretch as she bent her knees, and she concentrated hard on getting the position absolutely right. She saw that some of the other students were watching her, trying to figure out how good she was, and she willed her body to stretch even further.

"Your heels should be touching, Alice," Mrs. Franklin said as she walked along, checking to be sure everybody's positions were correct. "Lovely, Ellie. Very nice. Turn your legs out more, Michael, right from the hip. That's it. Everybody got their hips and shoulders level? Okay. Now into *demi-plié*—heels stay on the floor as you slowly bend your knees. Upper thighs turned out as much as you can manage."

Ellie breathed deeply and bent into position.

"Beautiful! Hold that stretch," came Mrs. Franklin's voice. "Now into *grand plié*. Let the heels lift as you bend all the way down. Thighs parallel with the floor, Bethany. And . . . slowly come up again. Heels down as soon as you can."

After their *pliés*, the class practiced a series of *tendus*.

"And now, I'm going to show you a *retiré*," said Mrs. Franklin. "This is a new movement that forms the beginning of an exercise called *developpé*, which we'll do another time. Does anybody know what *retiré* means?"

Ellie raised a hand shyly. "Withdrawn, Mrs. Franklin," she said. She'd just learned *retirés* in her last ballet class in Chicago. From the corner of her eye, Ellie noticed a skinny fair-haired girl, who had watched her during barre work, roll her eyes and whisper something to her neighbor. Ellie felt herself blush. Did the girl think she was a know-it-all?

"That's right, it means withdrawn," Mrs. Franklin said, smiling her approval at Ellie. "And this is how we do it . . . "

•   •   •   •

Before Ellie knew it, the class was over, and they were warming down. "Very well done, everyone," Mrs. Franklin told them. "See you all next week." She gave Ellie another wink. "Jolly good, dear. You've obviously been taught well. In fact, next week, I'd like you to stand at the front of the barre, near Bethany, so others can follow your form."

Ellie glowed with pleasure as she went to the changing room with the other students. She had always been the star pupil in her ballet class back home and was used to being praised, but it was still nice for a new teacher to single her out for a kind word. As she pulled on her sweatpants and sneakers in the changing room, the curly-haired girl called Bethany came over to her. "Hey, you're good," she said. "Really good. I'm Bethany Wilson, by the way."

"Hi," Ellie said. "Nice to meet you. I thought you were good, too."

The girl with jet-black hair and blue eyes came over to join them. "Hi, Ellie, I'm Zoe Matthews, Tasha's sister," she said. "Tasha's been telling me all about you."

"Hello," Ellie said, smiling back. Everyone was so friendly here! Well—almost everyone, she corrected herself as the skinny fair-haired girl looked over and gave her another cool, assessing stare.

Bethany started unpinning her hair. "You know, it's a real shame that you didn't get here earlier in the year, Ellie," she said thoughtfully. "Because you should definitely have auditioned to be a JA—a Junior Associate at The Royal Ballet School—but it's too late now for this year."

Ellie brushed her hair a few times before answering. "Actually, I came over in June for an audition," she said hesitantly, not wanting to sound as if she was showing off.

"Oh, yeah?" Bethany prompted. "And?"

"And . . ." Ellie started busily stuffing her ballet clothes into her bag to try and hide her face. "I got in." She didn't dare look up. The last thing she wanted was for anyone to think she was bragging.

To her surprise—and delight—though, Bethany started whooping and twirling around. "I'm one too!" she cried. "Excellent! We can go together!"

"That would be great," Ellie said. And she meant it, too. She felt a smile stretch right across her face and a warm feeling inside her. Maybe life in Oxford was going to be okay, after all . . .

Dear Diary,

I'm writing this in the bathtub—very carefully, so I don't splash the pages! I've just had my first class at Franklin's. I loved it there! I've felt like such a klutz at school, so it was awesome to be someplace where I knew what I was doing. For the first time since I got here, I feel like I fit in somewhere. Thank goodness for ballet!

I haven't told Mom that school has been a little bit up and down so far. I know it would upset her, and she's working so hard, preparing stuff to teach in her classes, even though the university term hasn't started yet. She seems really happy. And still no MS attacks!

Chapter 3

"Gee, if it ain't l'il old Tippitoes. Howdy, pardner!"

Ellie tried not to sigh. She and Phoebe had just walked into the playground, and there was Rachel talking with a crummy American accent. Not exactly the best way to start a school day.

Phoebe burst out laughing. "That is the *worst* American accent I've ever heard, Rach."

Ellie tried to make a joke out of it, too, and put on her most clipped English accent. "Yes, simply dreadful," she added.

But instead of laughing or even smiling, Rachel just turned her back to talk to somebody else. Why couldn't Rachel just let it go for once?

By the end of the morning, half the class was giggling at Rachel's exaggerated American accent, which she had insisted on using the whole morning. Ellie held on to her temper as best she could but couldn't help feeling a hot spark of anger flaring up inside her, like a lit match. So she had an American accent . . . so what?

At lunch, Tasha came up to Ellie and told her that Zoe had

said how good Ellie had been at Franklin's.

"Oh, thanks." Ellie smiled gratefully. "I—"

But Rachel interrupted and nudged Tasha. "Oh, I'd forgotten your sister was a Tippitoes as well," she said. "Don't tell me you're planning to be *Tasha* Tippitoes, are you?"

"No chance," Tasha laughed. "They wouldn't have me, for starters. I've got two left feet, if you hadn't noticed."

"Thank goodness for that," Rachel said. "I couldn't cope with two prima ballerinas in one class."

"I am NOT a prima ballerina," Ellie said defensively. Too late. Rachel had already stalked off.

"Don't let her get to you, Ellie," Tasha said with a sympathetic tone that somehow made Ellie feel even worse.

That afternoon, they played netball, a game Ellie had never tried before. It was popular in the UK, and kind of like basketball. You had to throw a ball through a hoop—but you weren't allowed to run with the ball or bounce it, and there were certain parts of the court you weren't even allowed in if you were a certain player, and . . .

Ellie's head was spinning with the rules. Normally, she was good at sports—she was a fast runner, fit, and athletic. Today, though, she was so confused by the game that she played it like a total no-brain and kept running with the ball or bouncing it like a basketball.

Of course, Rachel was a netball star. "Come on, Tippitoes, keep up," she bellowed. She threw the ball hard at Ellie, almost knocking her off balance.

"Hey!" Ellie protested.

Miss Welch blew the whistle. "I saw that, Rachel Travers!" she called from the side. "Any more tricks and you'll be off!"

Rachel glared at Ellie. "Trying to get me in trouble, Tippitoes?"

•   •   •   •

Walking home with Phoebe that afternoon, Ellie kicked at the fallen leaves on the pavement as she remembered the mean look in Rachel's eyes. What was her *problem*, anyway? She was nice to all the other girls. They all thought she was number-one funny girl. "Rachel doesn't like me," she said bluntly to Phoebe.

"Oh, she will," Phoebe said confidently. "I've known Rach since we were five. She's okay, really—she just likes to be the center of attention, and you, being a new face, have gotten in the way a bit. Just ignore her. She'll come round soon."

Ellie said nothing. She was starting to think that she didn't even *want* Rachel to "come round" and be friendly with her, anyway. Not after all this!

"Cheer up," Phoebe said, seeing the look on Ellie's face. She put an arm through Ellie's. "Everyone else thinks you're cool, anyway."

Ellie managed a smile. "Right," she said. "Thanks, Pheebs." Maybe Phoebe was right; maybe Rachel would get bored of teasing her soon. Boy, she hoped so!

•   •   •   •

On Friday, Rachel wasn't in class, and the morning went by much more quickly and easily. As well as Phoebe, Ellie was getting to be good friends with Ruby and Tasha.

In art class that afternoon, Ellie discovered that all four of her friends were as lousy at painting as she was. "Ruby, what *is* that, anyway?" she giggled, looking at the black-and-white smudges on Ruby's painting.

"It's a cow," Ruby said mournfully.

"It looks more like a penguin," Tasha snorted, sending her paintbrush skidding over the paper. "Oops—now my cat's got an extra-long whisker."

"Now your cat's got a black stripe on its tail, too," Ruby said, reaching out and dabbing black paint onto Tasha's painting.

"RUBY!" howled Tasha, leaning over and whacking her brush onto Ruby's paper.

Ellie and Phoebe were helpless with giggles.

"Actually, I think that looks better," Phoebe spluttered. "I reckon that cow was just crying out—no, *mooing* out—for a bit of brown paint."

"And that black stripe on the cat is sooo stylish," Ellie laughed. "Now listen, girls, I'm painting the Sugar Plum Fairy. And she doesn't want any black or brown, thanks very much!"

"Oh, I don't know, Ell," Tasha said thoughtfully. "A few brown swirls on that tutu would look divine . . ."

"Don't you dare!" shrieked Ellie, leaning forward to cover her painting. She giggled again. Her new English friends were crazy!

For the first time since she'd stepped through the gates on Monday, Ellie was enjoying herself at school.

Chapter 4

"This is Covent Garden."

Ellie gripped her mom's arm with excitement at the sound of the loudspeaker announcement. They were in London for Ellie's first Junior Associate class. It seemed like years had passed since they had been here in June for the audition. Ellie could hardly wait to get back into the wonderful Royal Ballet School's Upper School building.

Once they were out on ground level, Ellie smiled to herself. Covent Garden seemed like such a fun place to hang out. They passed a street performer dressed as a clown, juggling flaming clubs. On the other side of the street, a woman in a silver catsuit, her face and hair spray-painted silver, was standing very still on a platform as if she were a statue. Every so often, the woman would move and the crowd watching her would giggle and ooh and ahh.

A bit farther along, Ellie and her mom passed a couple of guys playing guitars and singing, and then they rounded a corner—and there it was. Ellie's heart practically stopped with excitement. "Wow," she breathed.

The Royal Ballet School's spectacular Bridge of Aspiration stretched above their heads. A twisted tunnel of glass and aluminum, it glittered and winked magically in the sunlight. It was just as awesome a sight as it had been when Ellie had first seen it back in June. The bridge went right over Floral Street and linked the school building with The Royal Ballet's rooms inside The Royal Opera House, opposite.

Ellie had to pinch herself to believe that this was really happening. It was almost too good to be true to think that she would be coming here, to the most famous ballet school in the world, every other Saturday.

"Goodness, Ellie, you've gotten very quiet," her mom said as they walked into the school's reception area.

Ellie blinked and then laughed. "I'm fine," she said. "Just feel as if I'm in the most wonderful kind of dream." She stood on tiptoe to kiss her mom. "Have a good time shopping, Mom. I'll see you later."

Her mom hugged her fiercely. "When did you go and get so grown-up on me, Ellie Brown?" she sighed. "All right, I'm out of here. Have fun, honey. And don't forget, I'm very, very proud of you." She kissed the top of Ellie's head.

"Thanks, Mom," Ellie said. Then she turned to make her way to the changing room.

As she entered, she caught the familiar smell of hair spray. Girls were gathered around a mirror, checking to see if their hair was in place. The others were pulling on their socks and ballet shoes, making sure the elastics on their shoes weren't twisted, or smoothing out wrinkles in their leotards. Everyone seemed to know one another, except for a couple of girls who looked a bit anxious. Other new girls, Ellie guessed.

"Hey, Ellie," said a familiar voice. "Want a hand with your plaits?"

Ellie spun around to see Bethany. Her curly dark hair had been neatly braided and was pinned across the top of her head with bows. As Ellie looked around the room, she realized that all the other girls had the same hairstyle, too.

"Oh, *braids*," Ellie said, patting her hair. "I didn't realize . . ."

"It's a JA thing," Bethany grinned, holding up a package of bobby pins. "You don't want to be a hair freak on your first day, do you?"

Ellie giggled. "No way," she said. She sat down to let Bethany fix her hair, relieved that her new friend had saved her from feeling awkward.

•   •   •   •

A few minutes later, as Ellie walked into the studio with the rest of the class, she felt a rush of adrenaline. This was it—showtime. Every single student in the room was going to be a great dancer, she reminded herself. They had all been picked out for their talent and potential, chosen from thousands of hopeful applicants to be JAs. It wasn't going to be like her old ballet school, or the Franklin Academy, where Ellie knew she was one of the best dancers, where she felt special. She was going to have to work harder than ever to be noticed here, where *everyone* was a star.

Ellie pulled herself up tall. She *would* shine. She was absolutely determined!

Their teacher was waiting for them. She was young and glamorous-looking, with her hair in a glossy black bob that swung whenever she moved her head. She was dressed in a black leotard and leggings and a filmy lilac skirt.

"Hello, everyone," she said. "I'm Ms. Taylor. I'm going to teach your JA class this year. For those of you who are new today, I know it must seem very overwhelming, the thought of dancing here for the first time, but as well as working hard, I want you to have fun. Don't worry too much about making mistakes or doing anything wrong. You're all here to learn—and because you're good dancers. It's my job to make you even better. Okay?"

There were a few murmurs in reply, but Ellie's mouth felt too dry to speak.

When warm-up exercises began, though, Ellie started to relax. They were the same ones she had done hundreds of times before, and her body knew what to do. So far, so good!

Once the class had warmed up, Ms. Taylor clapped her hands. "I'd like us all to make a *reverence*," she said. "I know this is something we usually do at the end of a class, but starting JA classes is an important step for anyone who is serious about dancing. I want us to mark your entry into the world of ballet, and think about how one day, hopefully, you will be making your *reverence* to an applauding audience."

Ellie and the other girls held out their arms, stretched one pointed toe to the side, then stepped onto that foot, placed the other foot carefully behind, and bent their knees in a deep curtsey. As well as a way to show thanks to an audience, the *reverence* was the traditional way that dancers thanked their teachers for their care and encouragement.

"Very nice," Ms. Taylor said approvingly. "Very nice indeed. Now let's make our way over to the barre."

After a series of exercises, the classical part of the lesson began.

They worked on the *croisé* positions. "The word *croisé* means 'crossed,' " Ms. Taylor told them. "Your body should appear as a crossed line to the audience." She moved effortlessly into the pose to show them. "Like so!"

Ellie gazed in awe at her teacher's graceful shape. She made it look so easy!

They learned that *croisé devant* was where one arm—"the upstage arm," Ms. Taylor called it—was held high, and the other arm to the side, and the leg nearer to their imagined audience held in front.

With the *croisé derrière*, the head was turned toward the audience, and the back leg was extended behind the body.

After the classical section came character class, where the boys joined the girls. The girls all put gathered skirts over their leotards and wore low-heeled character shoes.

"This kind of dancing is based on traditional European dances," Ms. Taylor explained. "Although it's not classical ballet, it uses the same kind of movements—you still need to stretch and jump and look graceful doing it! It's come to us from the long tradition of National Dance. If we don't teach it to young people, we'll lose it."

Ellie was partnered with a cheerful, wavy-haired boy called Matt, who danced really well—quick and light on his feet.

By the time class was finished, Ellie was hot and sweaty. She had pulled her body in every possible direction, and her leg muscles felt as if they were burning. Yet despite all of that, she was so happy, she wanted to *pirouette* around the room. It had been exhilarating to dance with so many other talented girls and boys at The Royal Ballet School!

Dear Diary,
   My first JA class today—WOW. It was sooo awesome. I can still hardly believe it. I, Ellie Brown, have taken a class at the actual Royal Ballet School! I can't stop saying it to myself!
   I think I must have done okay. Ms. Taylor gave me a pleased nod as we were leaving. It was like the best praise in the world! I can't wait to tell Heather about

it—there was an e-mail from her today with all the gossip from home. And I'm going to e-mail Ms. Lane, too. She'll know just what a big deal all of this is to me!

I'm trying not to get too carried away, but I can't help thinking how awesome it would be to study full-time at The Royal Ballet School next year! Students aged eleven to fifteen attend the Lower School at a place called White Lodge. Mom and I read about it on The Royal Ballet School's website back in Chicago. The school is in a huge park on the outskirts of London. Students live there and take ballet classes along with regular classes like math and science.

You know what? I'm starting to think it could really happen!

Ellie's high from her first JA class didn't last long, unfortunately. Rachel was back in school the following week, and she seemed more determined than ever to be mean to Ellie. They had played netball again, and this time, Ellie had remembered the rules and had done well. Her team had been playing against Rachel's team and won, thanks to two late goals by Ellie.

Rachel didn't like *that* at all. "Show-off," she'd said loudly.

"Oh, leave her alone, Rach," Phoebe had snapped in the end. "Give her a break."

But Rachel had just glared at Ellie as if she really did want to give her a break—a broken leg, maybe, or a broken arm . . .

· · · ·

Ellie was glad the school day was *finally* over. Once she reached her block, the sweet scent of the white roses climbing up the entrances to all the brownstones lifted her spirits. Oxford was starting to feel like home now. She couldn't believe how beautiful everything was. Each time she turned a corner, Ellie wanted to take another picture to e-mail to Heather. She loved the long green meadows running down to the river, the sun setting behind church spires and bell towers, and the glorious old colleges where, for hundreds of years, students had lived and studied. Talk about inspiring!

Ellie ran up the stairs two at a time and unlocked the front door to their apartment. "I'm home!" she yelled. "Mom?"

Ellie could hear the low buzzing of a radio, but there was no reply. "Mom, are you there?" Ellie called again. Silence. Had her mom gone out to the store? she wondered. Or maybe she was in the shower? Was the radio on too loud for her to hear?

Then Ellie heard a faint sound from the kitchen. Something clattering to the floor. "MOM!" she cried, racing down the corridor. "Are you okay?"

She hurled the kitchen door open, and a sob caught in her throat as she saw her mom leaning stiffly against the counter, white-faced and trembling. A smashed plate lay at her feet.

"I'm okay, honey," her mom said, forcing the words out. "Just a . . ."

Ellie was by her mother's side at once, arms around her, trying to still her mom's shaking hands. "It's okay. I'm here," she gabbled, trying not to sound as frightened as she felt.

Ellie's mom called her MS attacks "my tingling" or "my shakes," but Ellie knew it was more than that. Multiple sclerosis affected the whole of the central nervous system. Ellie had read up on it and knew that the symptoms varied from person to person. Her mom suffered from tremors, stiffness, and—if an attack was really bad—slurred speech, but Ellie knew that for other people, MS could mean hearing loss, terrible pain, and even blindness.

"Phew," her mom said, trying to joke as she gingerly straightened herself up. "It's going now. Sorry if I scared you."

"You didn't," Ellie lied, not wanting to tell her mother how frightened she'd been. She'd seen lots of attacks like this before, but it was still always awful seeing her mom unable to stop shaking. "Sit down, Mom, while I sweep up. I'll make dinner tonight."

"Oh, no, you won't," said Mrs. Brown, starting to sound more like her usual self. She smoothed back her hair. "Tell you what—neither of us will make it. Let's get takeout—maybe that Indian takeout on Tenniel Road? Is vegetable curry okay with you?"

Ellie smiled weakly. "Sounds great," she said.

Her mom already seemed to be recovering from the attack. It had been a mild one. But Ellie still felt gloomy as her mom hunted for the take-out menu. Her mom had been so *well* in recent months, it was a shock to see the MS back.

Ellie knew that there was no cure for MS—she knew her mom had it for life. Yet even so, recently she'd been hoping that it had become so mild, it was hardly worth thinking about. It seemed that she was wrong.

Chapter 5

"Stretch those feet, class!" called Ms. Taylor. "Str-e-tch!"

It was the fourth JA lesson of the term, and the class was working a lot harder today. Ellie stretched her feet out, right down to her toes. Sweat trickled down the sides of her face. And her leg muscles burned! *Stretch through the pain*, Ellie told herself. And to think that people like Rachel thought that ballet was all about prancing around in frilly, pink tutus! Any dancer who was serious about ballet knew that it meant years of hard, hard training, pushing your body to its absolute limits.

"Good work. We'll try a waltz next," Ms. Taylor told them. "Ellie, Bethany, Grace—let's have you three first, please."

Ellie ran to the corner of the studio and lined up between the other two girls. Bethany seemed like an old friend already. Ellie's mom hadn't felt up to the trip to London after her MS attack, so Ellie had come down on the train with Bethany and her mom. The two girls had chattered nonstop all the way from Oxford to London.

"And . . . ONE, two, three, ONE, two, three . . ." Ms. Taylor sang out in time to the piano music. "*That's* right, Grace. Nice work, Ellie. *Stretch* out, Bethany."

Ellie loved practicing the waltz step. It felt like a real dance. She and Grace and Bethany waltzed from corner to corner across the studio, then up the side—ONE two three, ONE, two, three— their soft ballet shoes making a *swish-swish* sound on the floor. She tried to hold her head up as Ms. Taylor had shown them, turn her legs out from her hips, position her arms correctly, and—as always—stretch her feet.

"Good," said Ms. Taylor, nodding with approval as they finished. Ellie smiled at her friends—a "good" from Ms. Taylor was worth all the hard work in the world.

Ellie walked over to the barre to wait for the other students to finish practicing the steps. She was exhausted—her skin was damp with sweat and her legs were trembling. *What a mess!* Ellie thought, grinning at her reflection in the mirrored wall. Wisps of blonde hair were sticking out in all directions, and the blue elastic waistband of her white Royal Ballet School leotard was twisted. Still, looking a bit sweaty and untidy at this point in the lesson wasn't such a bad thing. At least everyone could see just how hard she had been working!

Ellie watched the last group of girls waltz across the room. Ms. Taylor made them do the steps over and over again until she finally nodded and smiled. Ms. Taylor could spot a badly placed foot or a limp arm from across the room! She was a stickler for perfection.

"*Much* better, girls," Ellie heard Ms. Taylor call out. "You've danced very well today. Let's have a good *reverence*, shall we?"

The pianist began to play, and the dancers took their positions. They held out their tired arms and performed the *reverence* first to Ms. Taylor and then to the pianist.

"Before you go, I want to give you these," Ms. Taylor said, taking a pile of white envelopes from the top of the piano. "Would all of you who have your eleventh birthday between now and the end of August please take one?" she asked, holding them out.

Immediately, a buzz of excited whispers started up around the class.

"Application forms for the Lower School!" Ellie heard someone mutter.

Ellie felt the hairs prickle on the back of her neck. Lower School! So many brilliant ballet dancers had started out at the Lower School. And now Ellie was getting her very own application form.

The envelope felt heavy in her hand. It seemed a long time ago that she and her mom had looked at The Royal Ballet School's website back in Chicago and talked excitedly about Ellie herself maybe getting a place at the Lower School. But after her mom's MS attack the other night, Ellie didn't feel the same way about leaving her to go to boarding school.

Bethany's eyes sparkled as they walked to the changing room. "It must be the application forms, don't you think?" she asked breathlessly.

"Yes!" agreed Grace. "Oh, I feel sick with nerves already!"

"Tell me about it," Bethany groaned, fanning her hot cheeks with the envelope. "Can you imagine how scary the audition will be? Lower School is one of the hardest dance schools in the world to get into!"

Ellie stuffed the envelope into her bag. "It'll be far scarier for the applicants who aren't JAs," she reminded them. "You'll know much more about The Royal Ballet School than they will."

Bethany frowned at her. "*You'll* know much more about it?" she echoed. "Don't you mean *we'll* know much more about it?"

Ellie blushed and leaned down to take off her shoes. "Um . . . yeah," she said.

"You are applying, aren't you?" Bethany persisted. "Ellie?"

Ellie fiddled around with her shoes, hoping Bethany couldn't see the doubt all over her face. "I've got to talk to my mom," she said in the end.

"You've got to!" Bethany cried, *pirouetting* around the room dizzily. "I mean, just imagine it! Ballet lessons every single day!" She flung herself down onto the bench next to Ellie. "How *brilliant* would that be?"

"It would be cool," Ellie smiled, her stomach tightening. Oh, there was no doubt about it, it would be awesome, her dream come true, an amazing chance, but . . . could she really apply, knowing that it would mean leaving home, and her mom?

She and Bethany got changed, then raced downstairs to meet Bethany's mom. "Look, Mum!" cried Bethany, holding out her envelope.

"Is it the Lower School application form?" Mrs. Wilson asked. "I thought we'd get that soon." She took the envelope and put it in her bag. "We'll read it on the train," she said. "It's late enough already."

The three of them left the building and made their way through the crowds toward the Covent Garden tube station. As they neared the tube station, Ellie and Bethany saw Matt Haslum, the dancer who had partnered with Ellie at JA class. He was holding a familiar-looking white envelope. "Did you girls get your Lower School letters as well?" he asked.

Ellie nodded, trying to look excited. "Sure did," she said.

"Are you applying, Matt?" Bethany put in.

"Yeah, of course," he replied. "Everyone is."

Ellie felt her heart sink even further. She could hardly bear to think about Matt, Bethany, Grace, and the others all filling out their applications, going to auditions, maybe even receiving that dreamed-of letter saying: Yes, you've done it, you've got a place at the Lower School!

Matt was looking closely at her. "Everything all right, Ellie?" he asked.

Ellie nodded quickly, feeling herself blush again. "Yeah, fine," she said. "I'm just beat after today's class, that's all."

Mrs. Wilson put one arm around Ellie and one around Bethany. "Come on, girls," she said. "We've got a train to catch. And the sooner we get on it, the sooner you get to open your envelopes."

Bethany gasped and started to hurry into the tube station. "Come on, slowpokes!" she shouted over her shoulder.

.　　.　　.　　.

As soon as they were on the Oxford train, Bethany ripped open her envelope. She put the brochure and some forms onto the table and started sorting through them. "Wow, there's loads to fill out, Mum! Can we do it now?" she asked.

"Slow down!" laughed Mrs. Wilson. "We've got to talk to Dad first."

Bethany opened the brochure and peered hungrily at the glossy pages. "Here's a picture of a dorm," she said. "And look, Ellie, here's the Margot Fonteyn Studio. Big, isn't it? Oh, wow. Have you seen this?"

Ellie leaned across to see the picture of White Lodge that Bethany was pointing at. It had arched stone doorways and tall columns and was surrounded by trees and parkland. It was absolutely stunning.

"White Lodge was built as a hunting lodge in 1727 for King George II," said Mrs. Wilson, reading over Bethany's shoulder. "It has been the home of The Royal Ballet Lower School since 1955 . . . Isn't it beautiful?"

"I can't wait to show this to Mrs. Franklin!" Bethany said. "What do you think she'll say?"

Ellie swallowed the lump in her throat and forced a smile. "I think she'll say 'jolly good!' " she replied.

Bethany laughed and nodded. "Jolly, *jolly* good!" she repeated, sounding just like their teacher. She flipped over another page of the brochure. "Wow, look at them all in their tutus, Ell," she said. "Imagine being at boarding school! I hope we get in together. Maybe we can ask to have our beds next to each other. What do you think?"

Ellie didn't say anything, just smiled and nodded. She was worried she might do something embarrassing like cry. She rested her forehead against the window, watching the streets and houses of west London flick past as the train sped toward Oxford. Her eyes stung as she battled to hold in the tears, and her mouth ached trying to keep a smile on her face.

It wasn't that she didn't want to look at the pictures and read about life at the Lower School. She did—very much. But what was the point? How could she leave her mom to go there?

Chapter 6

When Ellie got home, her mom was scrubbing potatoes for dinner, and she wanted to know about the class. Ellie told her everything—and then, with an ache in her chest, she pulled out the Lower School application form. "Ms. Taylor gave me this," she said.

Ellie's mom looked puzzled. "You don't sound very happy about it," she told Ellie. "What is it?"

Ellie pushed the letter across the table. "It's just some stuff about the Lower School," she said. "But I'm not going to apply," she added in a rush. "Not while you're sick."

"Sick?" her mom echoed. "You mean that attack last week?"

Ellie nodded. "I don't want to leave you," she said. "It's a boarding school, and . . ." Ellie felt her eyes sting with tears again.

Her mom came around the table and held her tightly. "Hey," she said softly. "I'm managing the MS just fine, Ellie. And if I thought for one second that you were going to stay home because of me and not try to live your dream . . ." She broke off and rested her chin on top of Ellie's head. "I'd never forgive myself, Ellie," she said seriously.

Ellie leaned against her mom and felt the lump in her throat get even bigger. "Yes, but . . ." she started.

Her mom squeezed her even tighter, then turned her around to look her squarely in the eye. "Are you honestly telling me you don't want to apply, Ellie Brown?" she asked.

Ellie licked her lips. She couldn't lie. Her mom knew her too well. "I do want to apply," she found herself saying slowly, "but . . ."

"But nothing," her mom said briskly and tore open the envelope. She pulled the brochure and forms out and set them on the table in front of them. "And if you don't do it, I'll do it for you!"

Ellie threw her arms around her mom's neck and felt a rush of love engulf her. "You're the best mom in the world!" she said.

●   ●   ●   ●

After they'd cleared away the dinner dishes and Ellie had sent off an excited e-mail to Heather, telling her the news, she went into her bedroom with the brochure to read it all carefully.

As she looked around her room, she smiled. She and her mom had worked hard to turn the plain white room into a personal space for Ellie. They had painted the walls lilac, and Ellie had stenciled silver stars around the door frame. There were photos of all her old Chicago friends stuck on a big bulletin board on one wall and an enormous *Swan Lake* poster above her bed. Best of all was a barre along the longest wall that Phoebe's dad had helped install. But as much as Ellie loved her new room, she couldn't help wondering what it would be like to sleep in a bedroom at White Lodge, in a room full of ballet students!

Dear Diary,

I am soooo excited. I've just started filling out my application for the Lower School! It's all I can think about now. What must it be like to dance there— and live there?! Just the thought of being a full-time ballet student gives me goose bumps. Bethany said that students at the Lower School get the chance to perform with The Royal Ballet—THE MOST FAMOUS BALLET COMPANY IN THE WORLD!

Chapter 7

"Good news, Ellie! Mom says I can have a party for my birthday—with *boys*."

Ellie grinned. Phoebe was five minutes early for their walk to school—on a Monday morning, too. She must have been *really* excited for that to happen! "Cool," Ellie said. "So who are you gonna invite?"

Phoebe pursed her lips. "That's the problem," she said. "So far, my invitation list is ten girls and three boys. Daniel, Tom, and Joshua. They're the only boys I can think of who aren't complete jerks. Who else can I ask?"

"How about Zac?" Ellie suggested as they left the apartment block.

"Zac—ugh, no way! Are you mad?" Phoebe yelped.

"Joe, then," Ellie said, thinking of the shy, dark-haired boy who had helped her with a math problem the day before. "He's all right."

"Hmmm, but I don't think Rachel likes him," Phoebe replied.

Ellie felt a prickle of irritation. Why did Rachel have to dominate *everything*? "Well, Rachel doesn't like me, and you're still inviting me, right?" she managed to say evenly.

Phoebe squeezed Ellie's arm. "Of course I am, Ellie! You're number one on my list!" There was a moment's silence, then Phoebe shrugged. "It's just . . . Oh, you know what Rachel's like, though," she said.

I sure do, Ellie thought grimly. Rachel was *still* not giving her an easy time. Yesterday, Miss Welch had announced that they would be starting a class science project and would be working in pairs. Each pair was to carry out a series of experiments about magnets. "Now then, let's sort out the pairs," Miss Welch had said. "Phoebe—you can work with Ruby. Tasha—with Lucy. Ellie— you're with Rachel. Maddie . . ."

Ellie hadn't been able to hear another word. Paired up with Rachel? How awful was that going to be? Her heart had sunk even further at the scowl on Rachel's face.

"You'd better not mess this up, Ellie," Rachel hissed nastily.

Ellie hadn't been able to resist snapping back, "Same goes for you, too!" Just who did Rachel Travers think she was, anyway?

Ellie and Phoebe arrived at school just as the whistle was blown to go inside. They hung up their coats and ran into the classroom.

"Good morning, everyone," said Miss Welch, doing a quick registration. "We're going to start our science projects this morning. Please sit in your pairs and work through this hand-out together."

Everybody got up to swap places, but Rachel made no attempt to move. Instead, she slumped in her chair and gave a dramatic groan. "Do I *have* to go with *Ellie*, Miss Welch?" she said. "Can't we choose our own partners?"

Miss Welch narrowed her eyes. "You should be pleased to have Ellie as a partner," she told Rachel. "She's a very hard worker—unlike some people in this class. Now I don't want any more silliness, is that understood?" she said in her most no-nonsense voice.

"Yes, Miss Welch," Rachel muttered.

But she still glared at Ellie as they sat at a table together.

•   •   •   •

Ellie was glad when it was Wednesday evening and time for her ballet class at Franklin's.

"Everyone, take second position, please!" Mrs. Franklin called. *"Pliés!"*

Ellie was at her usual place at the barre—second from the front, behind Bethany. She turned her feet outward and placed them apart. She rested one hand lightly on the barre and extended her other arm gracefully. The music began, and the line of dancers bent their knees and lowered their bodies slowly and gently.

"Smoothly, please," called Mrs. Franklin. "No jerky movements!"

Ellie could feel the muscles on the insides of her thighs

working as she did her *demi-pliés*. Gradually, the rhythm of the familiar exercise began to push other thoughts out of her mind.

Mrs. Franklin walked about the room, calling out corrections and words of praise to each dancer. "Lovely head, Nicola! Watch those knees, Chloe—turn them *out*! That's it!" She stopped beside Ellie. "Jolly good!" she said approvingly.

Ellie glowed with pride. She caught the fair-haired girl, Nicola, giving her another of her snooty looks, but she didn't care. Ellie just grinned at her, and Nicola, taken aback at Ellie's reaction, turned her face away.

As barre work continued, Ellie had to take off her sweatshirt and leg warmers. Soon everyone else did, too, and the students formed a line of synchronized black leotards. Mrs. Franklin was very strict about the pupils wearing black leotards and pink sweatshirts, but they were allowed to wear any color shoes, socks, tights, and leg warmers they wanted.

Ellie found the familiar routine at Mrs. Franklin's comforting, and by the time they did their *reverence* to mark the end of class, she felt tired but happy. *Never mind Rachel*, she thought. She had ballet.

Chapter 8

The following day, Phoebe handed Ellie her party invitation on the way to school. "I've *finally* got my guest list sorted out," she said, sighing with relief. "Ten girls and six boys is okay, don't you think? I mean, nobody's going to be counting, are they? And I honestly don't like any more boys than that."

"Ten girls and six boys is fine," Ellie assured her. "But have you decided what you're going to *wear* yet?" she teased.

Phoebe pulled a pained expression. "No, no, no, absolutely no," she wailed. "Don't even *ask* me about that! I'm still stressing about decorations for the living room—are balloons too babyish?"

Ellie wished her biggest problem was decorating for a party! The minute she sat down at her desk, her stomach started to feel queasy. Since she'd been assigned to work with Rachel, science class had become her *least* favorite part of the day. And today, science class was first. After telling Ellie not to mess up their magnet experiment, Rachel now seemed completely uninterested in it. In fact, she seemed quite happy to let Ellie do all the work while she gossiped with the other girls about the soap opera they'd all watched the night before.

Ellie gritted her teeth and got on with it—for about ten minutes, anyway. Then she lost her patience. Why should she have to do all the work? Rachel must think she was some kind of sucker! "Rachel, are you going to do any of these tests?" she prompted.

Rachel's eyes widened at Ellie's question. "Oooh, look at Miss Teacher's Pet here," she said. "Don't get your tutu in a twist, Twinkletoes. I was only talking to my *friends*. But then you wouldn't know about that, seeing as you don't have any."

"I do, too!" Ellie snapped back, fuming.

"Girls, are you working over there?" Miss Welch asked pointedly.

Without another word, Rachel turned away from the other girls and sat down next to Ellie, grabbing a magnet out of Ellie's fingers.

"Hey," Ellie protested.

Rachel shot her an angry look. "Do you want to do this stupid experiment or *what*?" she snapped.

· · · ·

When it was time for Ellie's next JA lesson, Ellie's mom drove her and Bethany to London for it. She'd just received her British driver's license and had bought a secondhand car.

"So who do you think the real BADs are in class?" Bethany asked as they powered down the highway.

Ellie blinked. "The *what*?" she asked. She felt like she'd

never learn all of the slang!

"The BADs," Bethany said, grinning. "B-A-D. It stands for Brilliantly Awesome Dancers. Don't you know *anything*, Ellie Brown?"

Ellie laughed. "BADs—I like it. Hmmm," she said thoughtfully. "I suppose Grace. And Anna. And Matt's good, too, isn't he?" She elbowed her friend jokingly. "And of course, us two!"

Bethany batted her eyelashes. "Goes without saying," she agreed.

Ellie looked out the car window happily, wondering what they were going to learn today. She hoped that she would dance well enough to make Ms. Taylor think she was a BAD, too!

•　　•　　•　　•

Halfway through the class, Ellie caught Bethany's eye. "You are such a BAD!" Bethany was mouthing at her.

Ellie grinned back. She knew that Bethany was joking, but the class was going especially well today. Her barre exercises had been great, and her legs and arms were doing exactly what Ellie wanted them to do. Now they were working in the center of the room, practicing their *pirouettes*. Her legs felt strong and supple, and she had so much energy!

"And finish in *demi-plié*, arms *bras bas*," said Ms. Taylor. "Very nice, Ellie." As she walked across the studio, her chiffon ballet skirt swished against her legs.

Ellie watched her in admiration. Ms. Taylor had been a dancer in The Royal Ballet before she began teaching, and all the JA girls wanted to be as graceful as she was.

"*Sautés* next," Ms. Taylor went on. "Get into position, please. *Demi-plié* in first."

Ellie was pleased. She loved jumping. They practiced *sautés*—the light, springing movement starting and ending in *demi-plié*—until Ellie's feet were stinging and her neck was damp with sweat. She knew she was jumping well, higher than usual. Her leg muscles felt stretchy and loose, as if they were made of elastic and would carry her as high as the ceiling if she wanted them to.

> Dear Diary,
>   JA class was wonderful today. Everyone is getting really excited about their Lower School applications. I'd been feeling nervous, wondering whether or not I'd get an audition, but Ms. Taylor told us that everyone who applies gets a Preliminary Audition. So I'll definitely get to go and try out, at least!
>   I got an e-mail from Heather today. Here's what she said:

Hi, Ellie!

I miss you soooooo much! I can't believe you're actually in England. Does it look like it does in the movies? When are you sending pictures?

Libby and I went shopping today with my mom, and we got matching necklaces. They're hearts with little flowers in the middle. We're going to wear them to school tomorrow because we have to get dressed up for a field trip to the museum. I love field trips!!! Even the bus ride is fun! I wish you were coming with us.

Hope your dance classes are still going well, and don't forget about all of us when you're a famous ballerina. :)

Love,

Your Best Friend Forever

She seems to be hanging out with Libby a lot these days. I know it's crazy to feel jealous, but I couldn't help remembering how it used to be me and Heather who did everything together. I love it that we can e-mail each other all the time, but it's not the same as seeing each other. Who knows when that will be?

Chapter 9

"Are you *sure* balloons don't look babyish?" Phoebe fretted, glancing at the bunch she'd just tacked up in the living room.

"We're SURE!" chorused Ellie, Tasha, and Maddie, rolling their eyes at one another. For a laid-back, sunny person, Phoebe was very stressed out about her party decorations!

It was Monday—the day of Phoebe's birthday party—in Half Term, the weeklong mid-semester vacation in October. Ellie, Tasha, and Maddie were all helping to get the living room ready. They pushed back the sofas to make a good space for dancing, moved all of Mrs. Minton's breakables safely into the kitchen, and hung up balloons and party streamers.

Mr. and Mrs. Minton had prepared plates of sandwiches and cupcakes, and there were bowls of potato chips, grapes, miniature sausages, and chocolate chip cookies—all of Phoebe's favorite things.

Rachel was one of the first to arrive, looking great in a black cropped top, jeans, and black boots, with a silver flower clip in her hair and silver bangles on her arms. But as usual, she had a spiteful word for Ellie. "I see you haven't changed into your party clothes yet," she said, tossing her hair back.

Ellie looked down at her own outfit—a white, peasant-style top and a denim skirt—and instantly felt frumpy. *Just like Rachel wants me to feel*, she thought. "And I see *you* haven't changed your attitude for the party yet," she replied tightly, and went over to say hi to Ruby.

Ellie's skin prickled with annoyance. Why did Rachel always try to make her feel like an outsider? And why did Ellie always let Rachel get to her?

"I love that skirt," Ruby said, completely unaware of Rachel's insult, and Ellie didn't know whether to laugh or cry. She avoided Rachel for the rest of the party, though—and Rachel avoided her right back.

.   .   .   .

The following day, Ellie and Bethany went to Mrs. Franklin's to have their photos taken for their application forms. Mrs. Franklin had been really excited to hear that both of her star pupils would be applying to the Lower School and wanted to help in any way that she could.

She made them stand in four different poses, making minute adjustments before she took each photo. "I'll have them ready for you at Wednesday's class," she promised.

On Thursday, after school, Ellie put her photos in the envelope with the completed application form and sealed it. There. Finished!

Mrs. Brown looked at her watch. "If you take it down to the mailbox, you'll just catch the last collection," she said.

"Brilliant!" Ellie replied.

Her mom laughed. "You and your 'brilliant,' " she said. "You're beginning to sound as English as your dad these days!"

"Am I?" Ellie asked, feeling startled. Her mom sometimes said she looked like her father, if she was concentrating hard. It was funny to think she might sound like him now, as well. She loved to think there was still some sort of connection between them, even though she had only the vaguest memories of him.

It was a mild day in October, and the sun was shining. Ellie felt like dancing her way to the nearby red mailbox, she was so happy.

The mailman was emptying the box when she got there, so she held out the envelope. "Can I give this to you, please?" she asked.

The mailman straightened up. "Of course you can," he replied, smiling. "Looks important."

"It is," said Ellie, blushing. "Thank you!"

Dear Diary,

Okay, so the forms have gone in the mail. I wonder how long we'll have to wait to find out the date of the auditions?

It was Halloween yesterday, which was fun. Miss Welch passed out candy to everyone in the class. I missed trick-or-treating with Heather, though. I wonder what her costume was this year? I bet she went with Libby this time. It's a weird thought. I remember last year when we were both dressed up as wicked witches, and everyone thought we were sisters. It seems so long ago. I can't believe I haven't had time to e-mail her and find out this week. Everything has been crazy lately. I promise I'll do that tomorrow!

As Ellie came down the stairs for breakfast a couple of days later, she heard her mom's voice outside the front door, and then her mom came in with the mail.

"What were you doing outside?" Ellie asked.

"Oh, just talking to the mailman," said Ellie's mom, blushing. "Look, something's come from The Royal Ballet School!"

Ellie had the distinct feeling that her mom had just changed the subject. But she was too excited about the envelope from The Royal Ballet School to ask her any more about it.

Ellie quickly tore open the envelope. Her heart was pounding. She pulled the letter out and unfolded it.

There it was, in black-and-white: She had been invited to attend a Preliminary Audition at the Upper School building in Covent Garden on Saturday, January 18.

"YESSSSS!" Ellie cheered. She was so excited, she had to read the letter all over again. Then she made her mom read it, too!

"I wonder what they'll ask you to do?" Mrs. Brown said.

"Oh, it's like a regular class—only there are people watching you and giving you marks," Ellie replied, remembering what Ms. Taylor had told them. She shivered in anticipation, and started checking the letter for a third time. "We have to wear ordinary leotards, not white JA ones," she said, reading out loud. "Mom, I'm so excited!"

Just then, the doorbell rang. It was Phoebe. "Come on, Ellie!" she said. "We're going to be late!"

"Oops! Sorry, Pheebs!" Ellie said, looking at her watch. They should have left five minutes ago. "But wait until you hear my excuse. It's sooo good!" She kissed her mom, and they hurried off down the road.

"I saw your mum talking to the postman. Do you think she's trying to impress him or something?" said Phoebe, after Ellie had told her about the letter. "She looked really pretty with her hair all done and that new top."

"Phoebe!" exclaimed Ellie. "Are you nuts? Why would she be dressing up for the mailman?"

"I don't know—he's kind of cute, don't you think?" replied Phoebe, giving Ellie a teasing nudge.

"No, I do not. And neither does my mom!" Ellie insisted. "So quit matchmaking!" She forced out a laugh, even though she didn't feel like laughing. For some reason, Phoebe's comment had gotten right under her skin. She didn't want to think about her mom like that. Since Ellie's dad had died eight years ago, her mom had never been on a single date, and Ellie kind of liked it that way. Just the two of them. She knew it was a little bit selfish—wanting to keep her mother all to herself—but she couldn't help it.

Ellie didn't say much for the rest of the walk to school, but she was thinking hard. Phoebe was right: Ellie's mom had started to make a special effort to look her best in the mornings. But surely she didn't have a crush on the mailman?!

Did she?

Chapter 10

At school that morning, Miss Welch had the class making Advent calendars, which meant cutting tiny door shapes and matching them up to pictures on a separate sheet of card underneath. She'd asked them to draw or paint twenty-four little Christmas pictures, and Ellie and her friends were struggling to come up with even half that number!

"Do you think painting Mrs. Claus is stretching things?" Ellie joked. She'd come up with seventeen ideas for pictures but was struggling on the last few.

"It's *totally* stretching things," Tasha replied, her blue eyes twinkling. "Hey, Ell—what would you say this was?"

"Not another cow, is it?" Ellie teased.

Phoebe and the others started hooting with laughter. "Whoever heard of a Christmas *cow*?" snorted Phoebe.

"What's so funny?" Rachel wanted to know, strolling over to their table.

"Ellie thought my reindeer was a cow," Tasha said, pretending to pout across the table at Ellie.

Rachel didn't join in the laughter like the others, though. "Ellie's a bit strange, isn't she?" she said. "Whoever heard of a cow with antlers?"

Ellie held her tongue as Rachel went back to her own table, leaving an uncomfortable silence. Everyone else had thought it was funny. Why did Rachel always have to be against her? Ellie gritted her teeth and stared at her paper.

"Are you all right?" Ruby asked in a low voice.

Ellie nodded, pretending to be thinking hard about her next picture. "How about a turkey then?" she said, determined to keep her voice artificially bright and cheerful. She wouldn't let anyone know how much Rachel was getting to her. She just *wouldn't*!

. . . .

When Ellie got to Mrs. Franklin's on Wednesday, she could tell by the way Bethany was happily twirling around in the changing room that she had gotten a letter about the audition, too. "I'm so excited! I can't believe this is happening!" she cried when she saw Ellie.

"I know!" Ellie laughed. "But when I opened the letter, I was so nervous, I could hardly read the words!"

Most of the other students were pleased for Ellie and Bethany. "Promise us you'll remember *every* detail to tell us!" begged Jacqueline.

"You must be sooo excited!" breathed Zoe.

As usual, Nicola, the girl who had always been unfriendly to Ellie, had something mean to say. "You do realize that they audition loads and loads of people, don't you?" she said primly, pulling on her shoes. "I wouldn't get your hopes up too high. It's not like you're in the Lower School yet."

"Jealous, are we?" Bethany asked sweetly, and Nicola's cheeks flushed.

"Oh, I'm pleased for *you*, Bethany," she said. "But Ellie hasn't been in this country for five minutes! It's hardly fair, is it? I mean—"

"What's that got to do with anything?" Ellie asked. She wished Nicola would shut up! "The Royal Ballet School takes students from all over the world! They won't care how long I've been here."

"Ignore her," Bethany said. "She's crazy—and jealous because you're a better dancer than she is. Let's warm up."

Nicola's cheeks flushed even deeper scarlet and she turned away.

Ellie concentrated harder than ever during class that evening, trying to perfect her every step and turn. Afterward, Mrs. Franklin kept her and Bethany back. "What do you say to dancing solos this year in the Christmas Show, girls?" she asked.

Ellie and Bethany looked at each other. Bethany's mouth was open in shock, but no sound came out. Mrs. Franklin must have been really pleased with their dancing to suggest that they could perform solos!

"Yes, solos," Mrs. Franklin repeated. "And perhaps the two of you could perform a duet together? It'll mean extra work," she warned. "The show is in about six weeks, so you'll have a lot to learn if you're going to perform solos as well as with your class. Will you come to lessons on Mondays, just the two of you, as well as class on Wednesdays from now until the show?"

"Yes!" said Ellie and Bethany together.

"You bet," added Ellie, with feeling. The more practice she and Bethany could squeeze in, the better.

. . . .

The next few weeks went by in a blur of ballet classes, rehearsals, carol concerts, and Christmas shopping. Ellie felt like she hardly had time to eat, let alone think about the audition. The Monday classes at Mrs. Franklin's with Bethany were hard work, but they were also a lot of fun. Ellie loved watching Bethany practice her solo—she looked as graceful as a butterfly. And her own solo was going to be great, too. Ellie practiced hard at her own barre every free minute she had.

Life was so busy at school that it was almost a shock when Ellie realized she felt quite at home there now. She, Phoebe, Ruby, and Tasha went Christmas shopping together in Oxford one Saturday and laughed until they felt sick, thinking up silly presents they could buy people at school.

Ellie spotted a nail file. *Rachel would love that*, she thought. *Perfect for sharpening her claws!* She said nothing, though.

. . . .

The following Tuesday, the class was working on their science projects again.

"Oh, I hope you do well in your audition, by the way . . ."

Rachel said to Ellie.

"Uh . . . thanks," Ellie stuttered, caught off guard. Rachel . . . being *nice*? She was stunned.

Rachel looked at her. "Yeah, because then you won't be going to high school with the rest of us next year, will you? And we won't have to hear any more of your boring ballet talk!"

Ellie felt as if she'd been slapped. She couldn't believe she'd actually fallen into another of Rachel's spiteful traps. "You think I'm boring? Try listening to yourself, Rachel Travers," she snapped.

"Girls, if you're going to keep talking all through the lesson, you won't have time to finish your project," Miss Welch said. She had suddenly appeared behind them. "I want it handed in this week. And that goes for everybody." She raised her voice so that the rest of the class could hear. "If you can't get your projects finished in class, you will need to coordinate with your partners to get them finished in your own time."

Rachel and Ellie looked at each other. They were nowhere near finished writing their project. "I guess we'll have to meet up after school to finish it," Ellie said. She didn't bother hiding how unenthusiastic she was about *that*!

Rachel didn't reply.

Ellie gritted her teeth. "Why don't you come over after school tomorrow?" she suggested.

"I suppose I'll have to," Rachel replied, sounding glum. "If you can spare the time between *ballet* classes."

"For you, Rachel, anything," Ellie said sarcastically. "I can hardly wait."

.   .   .   .

The next afternoon, Rachel joined Phoebe and Ellie on their way home. It felt weird—and kind of awkward. Rachel wasn't saying much, but luckily Phoebe kept up her usual stream of chatter.

"Mum's taking me to the hairdresser's when we get back. What do you think—cut short or just a trim? Fringe? No fringe?"

"I think you'd look cute with bangs," Ellie volunteered.

"Bangs?" Rachel repeated.

"She means a fringe," Phoebe said.

Rachel rolled her eyes.

"But 'bangs' is such a cool word," Phoebe said, ignoring her. "I might ask for that, anyway. What do you think the hairdresser would say?"

"She'd think you were nuts," Ellie laughed. "And you are, Phoebe Minton!"

Back at the apartment, Ellie grabbed two bananas for her and Rachel to snack on, then they sat down at the living room table to start working.

"Is that your mum?" Rachel asked. She was pointing at a photo of Mrs. Brown that Ellie had taken at Christmas last year in Chicago. In it, Ellie's mom was wearing a pink party hat on her head and a couple of streamers around her shoulders. She was laughing into the camera. Ellie thought she looked beautiful.

"Yes," said Ellie shortly. She picked up her pen. "Should we start?"

But Rachel was still looking at the photos on the mantelpiece. "So which one is your dad? Is there a picture of him?"

Ellie paused, considering how to answer. She finally decided to go the simple route. "He died," she said bluntly after a few moments. She pointed to a framed photo on the wall behind Rachel. "That's their wedding photo. He died when I was little."

"Oh." Rachel bit her lip. "Sorry," she said gruffly.

The front door opened at that moment, and Ellie heard her mom coming in. "Hi, sweetie," she called. "Sorry I'm late. Had a flat tire on my bike and . . ." Her voice trailed off as she came into the living room and saw Rachel. "Oh, hi," she said. "Rachel, isn't it? Ellie said you were coming. I'm Amy, Ellie's mom."

"Hi," Rachel said.

Ellie watched Rachel carefully, her fists clenched under the table. If Rachel dared say *anything* obnoxious to her mom, she'd . . . she'd . . .

"Everything all right, Ellie?" her mom asked, coming over to kiss her cheek.

"Yeah, great, thanks," Ellie said. "Just about to start work on our project. Remember I was telling you about it?"

"Sure," her mom said. "Oh—speaking of remembering, I must take my pills right now. I was in such a rush this morning, I totally forgot. Then I'll fix you girls a snack."

Rachel was silent until Ellie's mom was in the kitchen.

Then she leaned forward. "What pills?" she asked. "What's wrong with her?"

Ellie's shoulders stiffened. "Nothing's wrong with her," she said crossly. Why did Rachel have to be so nosy?

Then a thought struck her. She didn't want Rachel to misunderstand—and go around blabbing to everyone at school that Ellie's mom was on medication. Knowing Rachel, she'd probably make something up. "If you have to know, my mom has MS," Ellie said tightly. "Okay? Multiple sclerosis. Now can we get on with this project? The sooner we start, the sooner we can finish." *And the sooner you can go home and stop asking all these questions about my life*, she thought fiercely.

She picked up her science notes and rattled them impatiently. "Anything else you'd like to know, or can we get started?"

To Ellie's surprise, Rachel shook her head. "Let's get started," she said quietly.

⋅　　⋅　　⋅　　⋅

The rest of the afternoon passed by easily enough. Ellie and Rachel worked hard on their project and managed to get it finished within an hour or so. Ellie felt really pleased with it. She and Rachel even shared a joke about how theirs was bound to be the best in the class.

As Rachel was waiting for her mom to come and pick her up, Ellie noticed that she was being very quiet. "What's up?" she asked.

Rachel chewed on a fingernail. "Ellie . . . I'm sorry," she said in a rush. She said the words so quickly, Ellie thought she'd imagined it. "I'm sorry I've given you a hard time at school," Rachel went on. "I got the wrong idea about you. I thought you were this . . . this dancing *princess* with a fairy-tale life."

"What? Dancing *princess*?" echoed Ellie in disbelief.

Rachel was scuffing her shoes along the carpet. Her hands twitched by her sides as if she didn't know what to do with them. "Yeah," she muttered. "Dumb, wasn't I? Now I know that's not how it is." Then she rolled her eyes in an embarrassed kind of way. "What I'm trying to say is, I felt jealous of you. And I kind of . . . I wanted to punish you." She hesitated. "And I'm sorry."

Ellie wasn't sure what to say. "Um, okay," she managed to stutter. There was a knock at the door. "That's probably your mom," she said, glad for the interruption.

Rachel pulled on her coat and picked up her school bag. "See you tomorrow, Ellie," she said. "And maybe we could . . . start again?"

"I guess," Ellie said, opening the door. She appreciated the apology, but she wasn't sure she'd be able to just forget about all of the mean things Rachel had said. "Bye, Rachel. See you tomorrow."

Ellie's mom came out of the kitchen to say good-bye. "Wasn't she sweet?" she said as the door closed behind Rachel. "I am glad you're making friends, Ellie. Now—what should we have for dinner?"

Ellie laughed. Sweet? Rachel Travers—sweet?

"What's so funny?" her mom wanted to know.

"Nothing," Ellie replied, feeling light-headed after the strange conversation she'd just had. "Nothing at all. How about baked potatoes and tuna?"

"Ellie Brown, I think you're becoming more British every day! I don't think you've ever asked for baked potatoes and tuna for dinner."

Dear Diary,

I am soooo tired! My legs and arms feel as if they're about to fall off. In fact, it's even an effort to write!! But it's been such a strange day, I need to get it all on paper.

First of all, Rachel apologized! I can't believe it. She seemed to have thought I was leading this charmed fairy-tale life. Yeah, right! And she made my life at school miserable just because of that! Anyway, once she knew about Dad dying and heard that Mom had MS, she seemed to snap out of it. She is the last person in the world I want sympathy from, so I feel a bit weird about it. But if it means she lays off, then I guess that's a good thing.

Second of all, we got to try on our costumes for the Christmas concert before ballet class tonight! For our solos, Bethany and I got to pick out tutus. Bethany chose a white one that looks really pretty on her, and I picked a beautiful pink one that reminds me of the one the Sugar Plum Fairy wears in the Nutcracker.

Ballet class was great, but sometimes (and I feel bad for saying this) I get jealous of Bethany. I can't help it. When she kicks her legs up so high in grand battement, she looks amazing. And she's so pretty—she looked gorgeous in every tutu she tried on. Mrs. Franklin always says that her personality really shines when she dances.

I'm worried that I won't shine onstage the way Bethany does. It's

terrible for me to think this, but I
know that I'll feel awful if Bethany
dances better than I do at the
audition. I'm ashamed just writing
those words down. Am I a really
horrible person for feeling like that?

Chapter

11

On Saturday morning, Ellie woke up and looked around her room. For some reason, it looked different. The lilac walls looked much brighter than usual, and the pink tutu hanging on her closet door seemed almost lit up.

Suddenly she knew what it was. She bounded out of bed and rushed to the window. "Wow!" she said.

The college gardens lay under a thick layer of snow, not deep by Chicago standards, but enough to play in. And Ellie didn't have JAs today, so . . .

"Mom! Mom!" she yelled. "Snow!" She dressed quickly, rushed through a bowl of cereal, then dashed across the hall to Phoebe's.

Her mom followed her out of the apartment. "I'm just going to pick up a newspaper," she told Ellie. "I won't be long."

"Okay," Ellie said, just as Phoebe opened her front door, still in her pajamas. "Phoebe—it snowed!" she cried. "Do you want to come out for a snowball fight?"

"Sorry, Ellie," Phoebe replied. "Mum's taking me Christmas

shopping this morning," she said. "Later would be great, though!"

Ellie felt her shoulders slump in disappointment. "I've got to practice this afternoon," she said. She loved having a busy life, but it did mean saying no to things sometimes.

"For the show?" Phoebe asked.

Ellie nodded.

"I was wondering if I could come to your performance?" Phoebe asked. "Could you get me a ticket?"

"Sure!" Ellie said, delighted that her friend wanted to see her dance. "You can sit with Mom. Oh, I'd love you to come, Pheebs!"

"Actually," Phoebe said thoughtfully, "could you get me two tickets?"

"No problem," Ellie told her. "Are you going to ask your mom to come, too?"

Before Phoebe could reply, they heard a cry from outside.

"That sounded like Mom!" Ellie gasped. She raced downstairs, followed by Phoebe, still in her pajamas and slippers. They burst out of the front door to see Ellie's mom being helped to her feet by the mailman.

"Are you okay, Mom?" Ellie asked.

"I'm fine. I just slipped on the step," she replied. "I should have put down some salt. You'd think I'd be used to snow by now, coming from Chicago!" She smiled ruefully, then winced as she tried to walk.

"You should sit down, Amy," said the mailman, looking

concerned. "Let's get you inside."

"Thanks, Steve." Ellie's mom smiled at him as he helped her back up the stairs to the apartment. "I'm not really hurt—just a little embarrassed!"

Ellie was surprised to hear that her mom and the mailman knew each other's names. And she didn't think she'd ever seen that look on her mom's face before—she had gone all pink and smiley, and she looked girlish, not like a mom at all. Ellie wasn't sure what to make of that.

Don't be silly, Ellie! she told herself as the mailman fussed around her mom, joking with her about being clumsy. *You're imagining things. Mom and the mailman are just friends. Aren't they?*

Once Mrs. Brown was sitting on the sofa in the living room and feeling better, the mailman left to finish his delivery route.

Phoebe got up to go home, and winked at Ellie.

Ellie walked Phoebe back to the hall. "Yeah, they definitely like each other," Phoebe teased when they were safely out of earshot.

"Pheebs! That's my mom you're talking about!" Ellie protested.

"Yeah, I know. But she *definitely* likes him," Phoebe said knowingly. Then she looked down at her slippers. "I'd better run before Mum finds out I've been out in my pj's," she said. "See you!"

Dear Diary,

I felt homesick for the first time in ages, seeing the snow today. I've been so busy lately, I've hardly thought about Heather, or Chicago. The snow brought back lots of memories of us sledding and making snowmen when we had snow days. I just love this weather!

I can't stop thinking about what Phoebe said about Mom and the mailman—Steve— liking each other. I don't know why it makes me feel uncomfortable, but it does. He seems nice and everything, but there's a part of me that doesn't want to share Mom with anybody. It's been the two of us for so long that it would be weird, having somebody else in the picture. Oh, no—jealous Ellie strikes again. I can't EVER let anyone see this journal!

The next few weeks passed like a whirlwind. Before Ellie knew it, the Franklin Academy Christmas Show had arrived.

As the curtain went up, Ellie and Bethany stood in the wings, dressed in their beautiful tutus, waiting for their cues. Ellie was nervous, but excited, too. She had worked so hard for this evening that she felt ready.

She peeked out at the audience while the younger class was performing. The youngest kids were so cute—but so clumsy! Occasionally, one of the little snow fairies bumped into one of the icicles, but Ellie could tell from the looks on their faces that they were having a wonderful time onstage. All the parents in the audience were smiling and gave them a standing ovation at the end.

Then Mrs. Franklin was out onstage to announce Ellie's solo.

Ellie's legs began to tremble, and her hands felt clammy. But as she stepped out to the middle of the stage, she felt a thrill. *Everyone's watching you, Ellie Brown,* she told herself, *so don't let them down!*

She raised her arms and positioned her feet. The audience was quiet. Ellie spotted her mom. And there was Phoebe, in her best dress, beaming at her.

Then Ellie noticed another familiar face next to Phoebe. Phoebe's extra ticket had been for someone Ellie had never expected to see there. Rachel!

Ellie gasped in astonishment as Rachel gave her a shy smile. Before she could wonder why Rachel was sitting there, Mrs. Franklin nodded to the pianist, and Ellie's solo music began. She was to dance a piece that Mrs. Franklin had choreographed especially for her—the dance of the winter fairy.

Ellie counted the beats in her head and began. She forgot all about the audience, and lost herself in the steps she had rehearsed so many times. Mrs. Franklin had told Ellie to go cat-watching to prepare for the many *pas de chats*—or "cat steps" in the piece. "Quiet, light, and stealthy—that's what a good *pas de chat* should be," she had said. "Study a cat or two—see how they do it!"

Ellie loved dancing *pas de chats*. It was a step that was in lots of her favorite ballets—like *Sleeping Beauty* and *Swan Lake*. She had to raise and bend her right leg rapidly to *retiré*, then, just as quickly, bend her left leg afterward, as if the left leg was chasing the right. "Don't just lift your knees up to your ears, *spring!*" Ellie could hear Mrs. Franklin's voice saying in her head as she leaped up high.

Ellie danced and danced, losing herself in the notes of the piano. Her arms flowed with the rhythm of the music, her legs felt supple and strong, her feet landed lightly on the stage after each step. She glided to the front of the stage and back, from side to side, the spotlight following her the whole time. As she *pirouetted* on the spot, Ellie felt like she *was* the magical winter fairy. She felt as if there were nothing else in the world but her and the music.

It was only the roar of the applause as the last notes faded that brought Ellie back to Earth. She blinked at the sight of all the smiling faces as the audience stood up, cheering and clapping for her. In the midst of her excitement, she nearly forgot to curtsey. The applause rang in her ears as she left the stage, and suddenly she was shaking with happiness. She'd done it!

As Ellie exited the stage, she saw Bethany grinning as

she waited in the wings to go on next. She gave Ellie the thumbs-up sign.

Feeling dazed, Ellie leaned against the wall to watch her friend from the edge of the stage. Anyone could tell that Bethany loved being on the stage, too. She wore a bright smile even through the trickiest parts of her solo. The audience clapped and cheered at the end as Bethany stepped into a perfect *arabesque*. Ellie had goose bumps just to hear them.

Then came their duet. They had magic wands, and sparkles to throw over the audience. It was awesome! Ellie couldn't think of when she'd been happier than dancing onstage with Bethany, with her mom watching from the audience.

Afterward, as she and Bethany got changed backstage, her mom and Mrs. Minton came to find them.

"You were wonderful, honey," Ellie's mom said, hugging her tightly. "I was so proud of you. I couldn't believe it was really my little girl, dancing so beautifully on that stage."

"Aww, Mom," Ellie said, trying not to blush. She didn't mind too much, though.

Moments later, Phoebe burst in, too. "Ellie, you were fantastic!" she cried. "Wow. I loved it. I absolutely loved it!" She turned to look behind her. "We both did. Didn't we, Rach?"

Rachel came into the dressing room. She nodded, an awkward smile on her face. "Yeah, you were brilliant. I had shivers just watching you."

"Thanks," Ellie said, shaking her hair out of her bun. "Thanks for coming." She smiled at them both. "Glad you liked it."

After Phoebe and Rachel had left, Ellie was hit by a wave of tiredness and relief.

Dear Diary,

It's late, and I'm really tired, but I'm still buzzing from the Christmas Show! Dancing onstage in front of an audience like that felt just so cool! Even thinking about it now makes me tingle. Mom said there was a photographer from the local newspaper there—and a journalist reviewing the show!

If only Grandma and Gramps and Heather could have been there, too! I missed them tonight. They always used to come to watch my Christmas shows in Chicago. Still, at least Phoebe was there instead. And talk about surprise—she brought Rachel along! I get the feeling I'm not going to have any more problems with Rachel now. I can't even begin to describe what a relief that is. No more Princess Tippitoes, etc.

Mrs. Franklin gave me and Bethany big hugs tonight and said, "If you dance as well as that at your audition, girls, they'd be mad to turn you down." Wasn't that sweet? She is just soooo nice! Only four more weeks to go before the Preliminary Audition! YIKES!!!

What else? I've been so busy with the end of the term and the show that my brain's turned to mush. Oh, of course—how could I have forgotten? Tonight, Mom said, "Wait till I tell STEVE about the show."

I said, "You and Steve seem to be getting along very well, Mom." I said it all innocently, even though I was totally fishing for gossip!

And get this, she went BRIGHT RED and said, "Actually, Ellie, I've been meaning to talk to you about that. Steve has asked me out on a date. How would you feel if I went out with him?"

I was so proud of myself. Even though I had been having all those mean feelings about not wanting to share Mom with anyone, I put my arms around her neck and pretended I thought it was a great idea. "If that's what you want to do, then go for it," I told her.

She was so pleased, I know I did the right thing. So why am I dreading them going out so much? And how weird will it be if they go and fall in love??? I'm not ready to have another father!!

Chapter 12

The next morning, Ellie didn't wake up until her mom had called her four times. Being a ballet star was exhausting!

It was the last week before Christmas vacation, and everyone was in a festive mood. There was a special mailbox in the school hall for students to send one another Christmas cards, and the secretary, Mrs. Daniels, delivered them to the classrooms every morning. Rachel sent Ellie one, and Ellie sent Rachel one back. Christmas was meant to be a time of goodwill, after all!

The whole of the last week was such fun, it passed by in a blur. There was an end-of-term carol concert and Christmas pantomime—a funny show acted out by some of the students and the teachers. Ellie's class also painted calendars and made glittery Christmas cards for their parents.

On Friday evening, Ellie's mom went out for dinner with Steve. Ellie stayed at Phoebe's. When her mom came by to pick her up, she seemed giddy. Ellie was glad her mom had enjoyed herself, but the thought of her mom going on a date was still strange. Phoebe was convinced they were going to fall in love, and

Ellie didn't know how to feel about that. It had always been just her and her mom for so long that the thought of another person joining their family seemed very odd. Part of her hoped that Mom *wouldn't* fall in love, but she knew that was selfish. Oh, it was so difficult!

•   •   •   •

On Christmas Eve, Ellie and her mom went caroling with the Mintons and some of their friends. They walked through the college buildings, then made a slow procession into town, singing underneath windows.

Phoebe tucked a mittened hand through Ellie's arm, and they crunched along the frosty cobbled streets together, singing "O Come, All Ye Faithful" and "We Wish You a Merry Christmas."

As the procession crossed over the river, Ellie saw the reflections of hundreds of Christmas lights in the swirling dark water below, and she felt completely in love with Oxford. It was just so beautiful! She gazed up at the spires of the old colleges ahead of her, glittering with frost in the moonlight. She felt as if she had stepped into a Christmas card.

•   •   •   •

On Christmas morning, Ellie woke with a smile on her face. Christmas! Totally the best day of the year, in her opinion! After a special pancake breakfast, Ellie and her mom opened the three packages that had arrived from Chicago.

One was from Grandma and Gramps and contained a framed photo of the four of them at a Cubs game. There was also a ballerina music box for Ellie.

The second package was from Ellie's mom's best friend, Jackie. She'd sent a couple of books for Ellie's mom, and a bag of Hershey's Kisses for Ellie.

"Good old Jackie!" grinned Ellie, ripping them open at once. "My favorite!"

The third package was one that Heather had put together for Ellie. She must have asked all of Ellie's old friends to contribute something, because the box was full of surprises.

Libby had sent a pink suede address book, which had all of their addresses written in it, "just so you don't forget us!" Ruth had wrapped up a pack of sparkly hair clips and hair bands, because she and Ellie had always had a running joke about how they were always losing theirs. Beth had sent a Chicago Bulls key ring. Shanice had written her a poem about friendship. And Heather had wrapped up a little blue teddy bear, who wore a T-shirt that said "hug me."

Best of all was a long letter from them, filled with gossip and news. Ellie felt a pang of homesickness at the familiar handwriting in the letter—followed by a guilty feeling that she hadn't been in touch much recently. She almost had tears in her eyes.

Her mom came over and hugged her. "Are you okay, honey?" she asked.

Ellie nodded. "I'm fine," she said quickly. "What should we open next?"

Once they'd unwrapped a few more presents, Ellie took a

shower, while her mom started making Christmas dinner. She was determined to follow all the British traditions, serving the turkey "with all the trimmings," as Phoebe put it: a chestnut stuffing, roast potatoes, Brussels sprouts, bread sauce—made from bread crumbs, milk, and spices—and gravy, followed by a sticky, fruity Christmas pudding and custard.

"Oh, Ellie, I forgot to tell you," her mom called as Ellie was dressing, "Steve is coming over for dinner. You don't mind, do you? His family is in Australia, and I didn't want him to be all alone."

Ellie shrugged. "I guess not," she called back. Her eyes drifted over to the photograph of her dad on her dresser. His laughing brown eyes and dark hair were so different from Steve's fair hair and blue eyes. "It's just . . . sort of a surprise, that's all."

"I know—sorry, sweetheart," her mom said. "I only asked him yesterday when I found out he'd be all by himself. I honestly meant to tell you right away, but my mind was so full of Christmas things . . ."

"Don't worry, Mom," Ellie said, seeing the apologetic look on her mom's face. "It's cool." Actually, now that she thought of it, Steve coming for Christmas dinner wasn't all that much of a surprise. The way her mom's eyes went sparkly whenever she mentioned his name, the way she had spent ages deciding what to wear before going out with him, the way she'd giggled to Phoebe's mom after their date . . .

No. Steve coming for Christmas dinner wasn't a surprise at

all. Ellie had just been ignoring the signs. But it looked like she wouldn't be able to ignore them much longer.

When Steve arrived, it was a little awkward at first. Ellie didn't know what to say, and she was unnerved when he kissed her mother on the cheek. It was strange to see her mom's whole face light up when Steve walked in and how she practically glowed when he kissed her. Ellie knew she should hug him—it was Christmas—but she wasn't ready for that. Steve was trying hard, though.

"Ellie, your mom tells me that you're a wonderful dancer," Steve said enthusiastically.

Ellie looked down sheepishly. "Yeah, I guess."

At dinner, things went a little more smoothly. Steve made corny jokes that Ellie's mom seemed to like. Some of them were funny. He really wasn't a bad guy. As much as she didn't want to admit it, Ellie did like him.

Dear Diary,

Merry Christmas, me! Today was "brilliant!" I got the black suede jacket I'd been hoping for, from Mom. And Mom really liked the book I got her about English painters.

Steve came over for Christmas dinner. I'm still not sure how I feel about him hanging out with Mom so much. He's nice and everything, and he makes her laugh a lot, and she seems to really like him, so . . . Anyway, we all had a great time.

Late afternoon, when it was mid-morning Chicago time, we called Grandma and Gramps and talked for ages! And then I called Heather, too. It was so cool to hear her voice. She made me promise to send her a copy of the clipping from the local newspaper with the photograph of Bethany and me in our tutus!

I hung the picture on my bedroom wall, even though it makes me feel a little silly to look up at myself. Hey, I've never been in the newspaper before! Every time I look at it, I remember how wonderful it felt to perform onstage. And I think about the audition I have coming up soon, and my stomach starts to churn. Oh, I so want to be at The Royal Ballet School!

Three weeks until the Preliminary Audition! I'm practicing every day. I just hope I can do enough!

Every morning between Christmas and New Year's Day, Ellie worked hard on her preparation for the upcoming audition. She would warm up and stretch almost as soon as she got out of bed, then move to the barre in her bedroom to practice her *pliés* and *relevés*, before moving on to different *battements*.

She found it helped to think of Ms. Taylor's voice in her head as she did them. "Start in third . . . into *coup de pied*, little toe just by the ankle bone . . ." she'd think as she practiced her fondus. "Swish that foot along and up in front," she'd think every time she did a *grand battement*.

She liked to practice first thing, so that she had the rest of the day to hang out with her friends, or her mom.

One day, soon after Christmas, the sales started in Oxford, so Ellie, Phoebe, and Ruby met up to spend their Christmas money on a few bargains and exchange news about one another's Christmases. When they'd all managed to snap up at least one new thing, they went to a coffee shop for hot chocolate and cookies, and made some New Year's resolutions together.

Phoebe wanted to go first. "I'm going to try to be less impatient," she said. "Like, right now, this minute!"

Ellie and Ruby rolled their eyes at each other and laughed. "That'll be the day," Ruby said.

Ruby went next. She vowed that she would stop biting her nails. "And we both know what your resolution will be," she smiled at Ellie. "To get a place in The Royal Ballet School—am I right, or am I right?!"

Ellie smiled. "You got it, Ruby!"

* * * *

On the first Saturday in January, Ellie and Bethany were back in London for their next JA lesson. It was nice to see all the familiar faces of their class again after the Christmas break, but Ellie's stomach felt tight and tense. The next time she'd walk through The Royal Ballet School doors, she realized, it would be for the Preliminary Audition.

"Only one more week!" said Anna, squeezing Ellie's arm when she and Bethany were in the JA changing room.

"My ballet teacher at home said to think of it as an ordinary JA class," Laura told them. "And at least we'll all be there to give one another support."

"I wonder where all the other applicants will be from?" said Bethany. "I mean, people from all over the world try to get into The Royal Ballet School." She widened her eyes. "I wonder if any of them will be BADs?"

"All of them, probably," Ellie sighed. "And just twenty-five or so places up for grabs." She grimaced, thinking about it. There had been twelve girls and thirteen boys chosen the year before from over a thousand applications. "We'll just have to try our hardest to be EMBADs, won't we?" she said with a determined glint in her eye.

"EMBADs?" Laura repeated.

Ellie grinned at her. "Even More Brilliantly Awesome Dancers!" she said.

Despite her brave talk, Ellie's tummy still felt tense as they began the warm-up exercises. Ms. Taylor had them all sitting on the floor to do some sideways stretches first. Ellie usually liked the simple elegant stretch of lifting up one arm above her head to reach right over to the side, but today, her body felt tight and inflexible.

"Keep your head aligned, Ellie," Ms. Taylor said, reaching down to put a hand under Ellie's chin and correct her position. "You need to follow the line of your arm, remember."

Ellie knew that. It was basic stuff! *Concentrate*, she told herself.

They moved onto some bending exercises, still sitting on the floor. "Feel your spine lengthening as you bend back," Ms. Taylor told them. "It should feel as if the front of your rib cage is lifting up from within."

Ellie's spine didn't seem to be doing anything.

"Hands on your knees, Ellie," Ms. Taylor said, and Ellie jumped at the words. What were her hands doing in her lap? She knew they were meant to be on her knees. Of course they should be on her knees! She'd been doing exercises like this for years! How come she'd forgotten something so straightforward?

It didn't happen often, but every now and then Ellie had a day when she didn't feel like a dancer at all. Mrs. Franklin called them "soggy" days and said that everyone had them. *But this is not the day to be having a soggy day!* Ellie told herself sternly. *You're only a week away from the most important ballet class of your life!*

The girls then moved to the barre to bend forward and backward. To Ellie's dismay, her body still felt as if it was struggling to do anything she wanted it to do. She watched Grace lifting her leg in *arabesque* elegantly and correctly—it was the best in the whole class. Ellie thought she'd never be able to do it as well, even on one of her best dancing days.

Laura, at the barre across the studio from Ellie, could bend and stretch farther than anyone else.

And there was Anna—she was just good at everything! Anna always knew exactly what they were supposed to be doing, and she learned new steps faster than anyone else. Her *petit battement*— beating your foot quickly, alternately at the front and the back of your ankle—was excellent: quick and precise.

"Face the barre, girls, for *echappés*!" called Ms. Taylor.

Ellie turned to the mirror, taking hold of the barre with both hands. As she placed her feet carefully, waiting for the music, she looked at her reflection. *Face it, Ellie*, she told herself. *You're not the best in your JA class. And that's not even counting the girls in the other JA groups around the country—never mind the BADs from everywhere else . . .*

Ellie pushed the negative thoughts out of her mind, and her barre work improved as the lesson went on. She began to feel a little better. Then it was time to work in the center of the room.

Ms. Taylor had decided to show them a new step. "Walk through it with me, girls, to make sure you know what you're doing," she instructed. "That's right, bring the arm through, Grace. Now, the back foot comes in, and . . . rest." It was a tricky step, with a Latin rhythm. Ellie liked the slinky feel of it.

They walked through it twice. "Good," said Ms. Taylor. "Let's do it in pairs, shall we? Ellie and Anna, you two first, then Bethany and Suzy from the other corner." Although Suzy was almost a year younger than Bethany, she was about the same size, and Ms. Taylor often paired them up.

Ellie and Anna set off across the room to the lively music. But when Bethany and Suzy followed, Ms. Taylor stopped them after only a few beats. "Bethany and Suzy," she said, "could you go back and try that again?"

They did it again. It was obvious to everyone what was wrong. Bethany just couldn't get the hang of it. They tried once more, and then Ms. Taylor showed Bethany the step again, more slowly. But Bethany just couldn't seem to get the rhythm. Her face was growing redder by the second. Ellie felt terrible for her friend.

Ms. Taylor calmly went on to the next pair, but Ellie could see Bethany was mad at herself. Her face stayed red all the way through character class, too.

Afterward, while they were getting changed, Ellie tried to reassure her. "Don't worry about it," she said. "It was a really hard step. And everybody has off days. Did you see the mess I made of the stretching exercises?"

"I'm *not* worried," Bethany snapped back. "I'm fine."

But Ellie could tell that she wasn't really fine. Her normally bubbly, talkative friend didn't a say word on the train back to Oxford. Audition nerves seemed to be making everyone suffer.

As she stared out the train window at the darkening sky, feeling her body ache, Ellie wondered how she and Bethany would be feeling the next time they were leaving London, after the audition. *A whole lot better than this, I hope*, she thought.

Chapter 14

Dear Diary,

I just can't sleep. It's past midnight, which means it is now officially AUDITION DAY. In just nine hours, I'll be on the way to the audition. OMIGOSH!

I know I have to go to sleep, like, now, but my mind is racing. What if I make a mess of the warm-up like I did last week at JAs? I bet I'll do something awful like lose my balance in the grand pliés. I'll probably topple right over—and skid across the floor, crashing into the examiners' table!

Mom went to bed hours ago, and the whole apartment building is silent. It's not fair! How come everyone else has managed to get to sleep, and I can't?

After some serious tossing and turning and pillow-plumping, Ellie finally managed to doze off. At seven o'clock, though, her eyes popped open, and she lay still in the warmth of her bed for a second until a single word slammed into her head. AUDITION. There was no going back to sleep after *that*.

Ellie got out of bed and stretched out on her bedroom floor. *Nice and easy, nice and easy,* she told herself as calmly as possible. Her body felt more willing and flexible than it had the week before. Good. That was something, at least!

Ellie showered and dressed, putting her black leotard on under her clothes. Then she looked at her watch. There was only another ten minutes before her mom would get up, so Ellie decided to get her mother's morning coffee started. Her mom always said she couldn't find her brain in the morning until she'd had a decent cup of coffee!

As she passed her mom's bedroom door, though, Ellie was startled to hear a weak, slurred voice calling from the other side. Heart thumping, she opened the door to see her mom sitting stiffly on the side of the bed, her nightdress twisted around her body. She was shaking.

"Mom!" Ellie cried, rushing over to help her back into bed.

"Your . . . Your au . . ." her mom began slowly, tears rolling down her face.

Ellie knew what her mother was trying to say. *Your audition.* "Don't worry about that," Ellie said. "I'm staying with you."

But her mom was sobbing now and holding tightly onto

Ellie's arm. Ellie began to feel really frightened. She'd never seen her mom this upset. "It's okay," she managed to say. "I'm here, Mom. Let me just go and get help."

Ellie raced down the hall and out the front door. She ran across the landing and hammered on the Mintons' door. But no one answered. She suddenly remembered that they had planned to leave first thing to drive up to Phoebe's grandparents for the day.

Feeling sick with panic, Ellie rushed back across the landing and into the apartment. *I don't know what to do, I don't know what to do*, she thought, almost sobbing with fear. She picked up the phone and dialed 999, the number for the British ambulance service.

"We'll send someone over as soon as possible," the operator told her after Ellie explained what had happened.

Ellie felt as if she was in a nightmare. She packed some clothes for her mom and then, with a sickening lurch inside, wrote a note to Bethany.

MOM SICK—CAN'T GO TO AUDITION.

CALL ME LATER.

She taped the note to the front door. Seeing the words in black-and-white made it feel even worse. She was going to miss her audition. Her Lower School audition!

She pushed the thought away as fast as she could. She'd have to think about that later. Right now, her mom was far more important.

The time it took for the ambulance to come was only a few

minutes, but it felt like hours. Ellie's mom was still shaking uncontrollably. Her eyes were glassy and bright, and her skin was clammy and pale.

It was a relief to let the paramedics into the apartment, even though it was scary seeing them pick up her mom and carry her down to a stretcher bed.

"Are you all right, love?" one of the paramedics asked Ellie, helping her up into the ambulance.

"I'm fine," Ellie said, brushing the tears off her cheeks. She *had* to be fine, for her mom's sake. Then she sat down in the ambulance beside her mom and held her hand all the way to the hospital.

Dear Diary,
 I'm in the Mintons' bathroom because I'm staying over at Phoebe's—in a folding bed in her room—and she's already asleep. But I really needed to write about this stuff now.
 Today was terrible. Mom ended up in the hospital. And I missed my audition.
 Mom's attack this morning was bad—her vision was blurry, and her speech was slurred. But what made it even worse was that she was so upset, too—because it was happening on the day of my audition.
 The doctors wanted to keep Mom in the

hospital overnight, but she'll probably be okay to come home tomorrow. She sure looked a lot better this evening than she did this morning, which was a big relief.

I can hardly bear to even think about the audition. I just can't believe I missed my Preliminary Audition for The Royal Ballet School. This time yesterday, I felt so ready! I was excited and just the right amount of nervous. But now it's too late. It's just too late.

Bethany's mom called me here tonight to see how Mom was. She is sooo nice. It has made me realize just how lucky we are to have made such good friends here. She said Bethany had guessed I'd be here, and she'd gotten the Mintons' number from the phone book. I had to ask Bethany how she'd done at the auditions, so Mrs. Wilson handed the phone to her.

Bethany said that she'd danced okay, and that Grace had danced awesomely and that all the other girls in our JA group had looked good. Laura and Anna had gotten a fit of the giggles because they were so nervous. Hearing that made me feel even worse that I missed out. Anyway, I know I did the right thing, staying with Mom. There was no way I was gonna leave her—not even for an audition. I've just got to forget the whole thing now, and move on.

Yeah, right. Like that's gonna be easy . . .

Chapter

15

Ellie's mom was pale and tired but feeling better when Mrs. Minton and Ellie went to take her home from the hospital the next day. They carefully helped her out of the wheelchair and into the backseat of the Mintons' car, and Ellie got in next to her.

As they set off, Ellie's mom turned to her. "Ellie, honey . . . I am so sorry about your audition," she said. "I'd give anything to change what happened yesterday. I wish you had gone."

"It's okay, Mom," Ellie replied firmly. She didn't want her mother to get upset again. "I'm glad I stayed with you." She winced. "It's probably for the best, anyway. I mean, what would happen if you had an attack like that, and I was away at The Royal Ballet School? It was a bad idea to apply in the first place."

Her mom pulled Ellie to her. "No, honey! Don't think like that!" she insisted. "It's terrible that you missed the audition because of my MS, but you *can't* think you can never leave me on my own. It could just as easily have happened while you were at school," she pointed out. "And I would've called Phoebe's mom or the ambulance by myself."

"Ellie, love, I'm just sorry I wasn't around to help yesterday morning," Mrs. Minton said from the front of the car.

"Thanks, Mrs. Minton," Ellie said. Then she turned again to her mom. "But . . . but who would make dinner and clean up while you're resting if I wasn't here?" she asked. "You wouldn't be able to do all that if you were sick."

"I know," her mom agreed. "But, honey, we have people here who care about us. Phoebe's mom is only across the way—she'd help out. And Steve could always come and stay." She kissed the top of Ellie's head. "You don't have to look after me all by yourself. You need to look after you, too!"

Ellie wasn't sure what to say. She fiddled with her fingers in her lap, and gazed out of the window. She felt too numb to think about herself right now. All she knew was that she missed her big chance. She'd blown everything.

.   .   .   .

When they got back home, Ellie went over to talk to Phoebe. Now that her mom was looking okay again, the reality of having missed her audition was sinking in. Ellie didn't want her mom to know how upset she was—that would only make her feel guilty. But she really needed to talk to someone about it.

As soon as the girls were safely in Phoebe's bedroom, Ellie burst into tears. "Everything's wrong," she cried miserably. "Everything's ruined."

Phoebe hugged her. "Oh, Ellie," she said. "It's so unfair. Can't you have another audition next week, or something? Is there anything you can do?"

"No," Ellie sobbed. "It's too late. You're supposed to show up for an audition unless you're ill or injured," she said. "And I wasn't either of those."

Phoebe rubbed her back. "I'm really sorry," she said. "I know how much you wanted to go."

"Mrs. Franklin was so excited that two of her students were auditioning for The Royal Ballet School!" Ellie said. Hot tears fell as she thought of her teacher's kind face. "She's going to be so disappointed when she hears I didn't even show up. And I don't know *how* I'm going to face Ms. Taylor at next Saturday's JA class!"

Phoebe shook her head. "They'll understand," she said firmly. "They will totally understand. It's not your fault. You did the right thing, Ellie."

Ellie pulled out a tissue, blew her nose, and tried really hard to stop crying. "Thanks, Pheebs," she said gratefully. "I did, didn't I?" She managed a weak smile. "What would I do without you?"

•   •   •   •

On Wednesday, Ellie just didn't want to go to ballet class. She wasn't even packed when Bethany and her mom came to pick her up. Bethany looked really nice, with her hair smoothed and sprayed, and new gold studs in her ears. Ellie caught sight of herself in the hall mirror. She looked exactly like she felt. All pale and pinched and crumpled up.

"Nothing wrong, is there, Ellie?" asked Mrs. Wilson, looking concerned.

Ellie shook her head. "Sorry," she said. "I'm just being slow."

"Don't worry, sweetheart," Mrs. Wilson said. "I'll say hello to your mum while you get ready." She went into the living room.

Bethany looked at her carefully. "Ellie, are you really okay?" she asked.

Ellie opened her mouth to say yes, then sighed. "No, not really. I don't want to go tonight—everyone will be asking questions and feeling sorry for me," she said. She shrugged her shoulders miserably. "I guess if I don't go tonight, though, I'll only have to face it next week—or the week after . . ."

Bethany nodded sympathetically. "It'll be fine," she said. "You'll see."

.   .   .   .

Bethany was right. To Ellie's relief, no one at Franklin's mentioned the audition. Zoe had gotten a new cell phone, and the other students were far more interested in that.

Ellie began to relax and enjoy the familiar feeling of her muscles working as she stretched and bent her knees in *pliés*. She felt her back straighten and her neck lengthen. She remembered to turn out and stretch—and noticed Rebecca, a new girl, copying her. Soon, she started to feel like Ellie Brown, dancer, again.

Dear Diary,
    I was really surprised that ballet felt so good tonight, considering I didn't even want to go in the first place. But I guess that

nothing can keep me from loving ballet. I was glad that Mrs. Franklin didn't say much about me missing the audition. She asked about Mom and said how sorry she was, but that was all. Anything more, and I think I might have cried.

It was strange, though—I caught her watching me really closely a few times—and frowning. I wonder what she was really thinking?

Just Ms. Taylor to face now. I am DREADING it . . .

Chapter
16

A couple of days before Ellie's next JA class, she was just coming out of the front door when she almost bumped into Steve. He gave her a white envelope addressed to her mom. It had The Royal Ballet School's crest in the corner.

"Thanks, Steve." Ellie was too nervous to give Steve a chance to speak.

She stared at the envelope, her heart thumping. What could it be about?

Then her excitement faded. It was probably just the official letter to say that, as she hadn't shown up, she'd automatically failed the audition. "Mom!" she called.

Her mother came out of the kitchen, smiling at Steve. "Hello, you," she said happily. "Are we still on for going to that new art gallery tonight?"

"Never mind the art gallery, Mom!" Ellie said. "Steve brought a letter from The Royal Ballet School. Probably just a thanks but no thanks, but let's open it."

Her mom took the envelope and tore it open. As she read the

letter, she began to smile. "It's from the Auditions Secretary," she said slowly. "But it isn't what you think." She handed Ellie the letter.

Ellie looked at her mom curiously, then began to read.

It *was* from the Auditions Secretary of The Royal Ballet School. It said that Ellie had been selected to attend the Final Audition, which would be held at the Lower School on Saturday, March 6.

"But—but—how?" Ellie gasped.

"Read the rest," said her mom, smiling.

The letter explained that Mrs. Franklin had contacted Ms. Taylor to ask if she could send a videotape of Ellie dancing her solo in the Christmas Show, since she had missed the Preliminary Audition through no fault of her own.

". . . and in view of the exceptional circumstances," Ellie read, "the Director agreed that Ellie could be selected for the Final Audition on the basis of the video."

Ellie's eyes were now so wide, the words started dancing around on the page. *The Final Audition!* She had been invited to the Final Audition! She'd been given another chance!

Ellie could hardly breathe. She read the words again and again, then bounded around wildly, cheering and laughing. She hugged her mom, then Steve, then her mom again. "I have to go tell Phoebe!" she cried, grabbing her school bag. "I want to tell everybody in the world!"

·   ·   ·   ·

The whole way to school, Ellie couldn't talk about anything

but the letter. "I'm so amazed at what Mrs. Franklin did for me," she said, beaming. "I'm going to get her some flowers to say thank you. Imagine, Pheebs, if I get in! Just imagine!"

"I *am* imagining," Phoebe replied quietly, looking at the sidewalk.

Ellie looked at her. "Are you all right, Pheebs?" she asked. "Sorry, have I been going on too much? It must seem like ballet is all I ever talk about."

Phoebe shook her head. "No, of course not—it's fab news," she said. "It's just . . ."

"Just what?" Ellie prompted.

"Just that I'll *miss* you. I feel like we've been friends for ages already." Phoebe's eyes were sad. "I mean, this is dead exciting, all the ballet stuff, and I'm really happy for you, but . . . I'm kind of used to having you next door, that's all. I can't imagine you not being there now."

"Oh, *Pheebs*," Ellie said, grabbing Phoebe's hand. "I'll miss you, too. I'll miss you tons. But I'll be back for the holidays and weekends—it's not like we'll never see each other again." Then she shook her head. "Anyway, I've got to get through the audition yet. With my luck, the car will break down before I get there, or I'll roll out of bed the night before and sprain my ankle or—"

Phoebe laughed. "Don't! Stop it! You'll be fine." She glanced down at her watch. "Anyway, come on, superstar, or we'll be late!"

Dear Diary,

I talked to Bethany on the phone after dinner, and she told me that she made it to the Final Audition, too! And so have Grace and Laura—but no one else from our JA class. I was really surprised that Anna didn't get through. Anna's brother didn't, either, but Matt Haslum, Oliver Stafford, and James Rock did. Oliver's a total BAD, so he's bound to get in. I hope Matt does, too. His family is moving to Birmingham, a city farther north, so he'll be doing the rest of this year's JA classes at the Birmingham JA center. I'll miss him.

One thing's for sure: Now that I've been given this extra chance, I am NOT going to waste it. I'll dance better at that Final Audition than I ever have in my life. Just watch me!

Chapter 17

One mild February afternoon, Ellie arrived home from school to see her mom sitting under the magnolia trees in the college gardens. The trees were covered with small, fuzzy buds.

Her mom held open her arms. "Come sit with me, honey," she called.

Ellie walked over, and as she drew close, she could see that her mom had been crying. And suddenly, she realized why. Today was her dad's birthday.

Ellie sat down and snuggled up to her mom, like she used to do when she was little.

"Your dad would have been thirty-nine today, honey."

Ellie nodded, resting her head against her mom's shoulder.

They sat there as the air grew chilly, talking about Ellie's dad. How he'd been a student at Oxford University and had offered to show Ellie's mom around when she'd arrived for a semester as an exchange student from Chicago. And how they'd spent all their free time together. And how he'd then followed her back to Chicago and asked her to marry him. And how they had bought the tiny blue-and-white house by the lake.

"Your daddy and Gramps worked so hard, fixing it up," her mom went on. "They got to know each other really well by the time they'd finished! And when you came along, we were so happy . . ." She sniffed again and wiped her eyes.

Ellie wrapped her arms tightly around her mom. She just wished she had more memories of her dad. She felt there was an empty space inside her that belonged to him. Was it possible to miss somebody you'd hardly known? Somehow, she did. She would have loved a chance to get to know him—to make him laugh, to make him proud. The thought of him dying before they'd spent much time together was too sad for words.

"You know, I think that your daddy would have liked Steve," her mom said quietly.

Ellie hugged her. "I think so, too, Mom," she replied.

They held each other tight as they sat there for a while longer, thinking about the past and the future, until it got too cold, and it was time to go indoors.

·   ·   ·   ·

The build-up to the Final Audition became more intense for Ellie and Bethany. Mrs. Franklin was giving them extra classes— and they were working hard. She urged them on all the time. Jump *higher*, reach *further*, show your *face*, where are your *arms*, stretch your back *foot*, land in *fifth*, think about your *line* . . . It was like a drum beating in Ellie's head.

At home, Ellie was stretching every morning before school and doing exercises every evening after she finished her homework. She felt like she was eating, breathing, and sleeping ballet—so much so that the days at school passed like a dream.

"Earth to Ellie, Earth to Ellie!" Phoebe had taken to joking. "Do you receive us on Planet Ballet?"

"Sorry, Pheebs," Ellie would grin. "What were you saying?"

.   .   .   .

On the last Friday before the audition, Phoebe handed Ellie a card. It said "GOOD LUCK!" on the front, and was signed by everyone in the class. Phoebe pulled out her calendar and pretended to consult it. "And I've booked you for a two-hour gossip about the whole thing as soon as you get home," she said, sounding stern.

"You bet!" Ellie grinned.

"Here's my good-luck bracelet," Ruby said, pressing it into Ellie's hand. "Look—a red stone, just like a ruby. You can borrow it—keep it in your bag, or something. It always works."

"Phone me, won't you, when you get back tomorrow?" Tasha asked. "I'm dying to know how it goes—and so is Zoe."

Even Rachel made a point of coming up to Ellie. "Good luck," she said. "And I mean it this time," she added, smiling a bit awkwardly.

"Thanks, guys," Ellie said. She felt overwhelmed by how kind they all were being.

She caught Phoebe's eye and saw that her friend was looking wistful all over again. It gave Ellie a lump in her throat to see cheerful Phoebe without a smile. Nothing was ever black-and-white, she thought to herself, feeling a rush of sadness. Getting a place at the Lower School would be a dream come true, but it would mean leaving behind her new friends, too. Why did everything have to be so complicated?

Dear Diary,

Tomorrow is the Final Audition. My bag's packed, my clothes for the morning are laid out on my chair—I've even planned what I'm going to have for breakfast! Now there's nothing left to do but go for it. I'm going to do it for Mom, Grandma and Gramps—and for Dad. I'm going to do it for Ms. Taylor and Mrs. Franklin and everyone who's helped me. I'm going to do it for Heather and the gang in Chicago—and Phoebe, Tasha, and Ruby, and all my other English friends who are rooting for me.

Most of all, though, I'm going to do it for ME!

"Do you think that lucky charms really work?" Bethany asked, twisting a silver ring around her middle finger anxiously.

"I hope so," Ellie said, patting the bracelet that Ruby had lent her. "I've brought about five with me."

It was the day of the Final Audition. Ellie was in the Wilsons' car with her mom, Bethany, and Bethany's parents. They were just arriving in Richmond Park, on the edge of southwest London. White Lodge was in the middle of the park, and the only way to get there was by car or by taxi from Richmond station.

Bethany laughed. "Only five? I reckon I've got at least seventeen!"

"If they get us into the Lower School, then who cares?" Ellie said, gazing out the window. Her eyes widened as she spotted a herd of deer gathered in the shade of a clump of trees. "Look!" she cried. "Deer!"

Ellie was surprised by how huge Richmond Park was. The grass and trees seemed to go on forever, and there were no flowerbeds or fountains like in a regular city park. It felt more like open countryside. And now she'd just seen deer, in London!

They drove up a hill, then over a cattle grid. A man in a yellow plastic vest at the side of the road checked their names and waved them on, and then suddenly, White Lodge came into view.

Ellie had seen pictures of White Lodge—she had stared at the ones in the brochure until her eyes hurt! But photos hadn't prepared her for this majestic building. Its enormous, pale stone columns shone under the March sunlight, and there were rows of high windows and heavy wooden double doors.

"Wow," Bethany said, wide-eyed, and Ellie nodded in agreement, utterly speechless.

As they collected the bags from the trunk, Mrs. Brown squeezed Ellie's hand. "Don't be intimidated by how grand the building is, honey," she whispered. "It's only bricks and mortar. All that matters is that you dance your best."

Ellie nodded. "I know," she said, giving her mom a quick hug.

As they went into the reception room, Ellie gazed at the rows of black-and-white photographs on the walls. There were her heroes and heroines—Dame Antoinette Sibley and Sir Anthony Dowell, Darcey Bussell, Dame Margot Fonteyn. WOW. Suddenly, she felt struck dumb with nerves.

The girls and their families were directed through a set of doors and past a bronze statue of Dame Margot Fonteyn. "Look," Bethany whispered. "See that really shiny finger on her hand there? I read somewhere that all the students touch it for luck!"

"I wish you had told me that before we passed it! I could have used a little extra luck," Ellie said with a nervous giggle.

The Browns and the Wilsons were taken through to a more modern building on the grounds of the old house. There, they were greeted by a cheerful lady whose badge said "Pamela Dale, Auditions Secretary." She checked their names on her list and gave Ellie and Bethany numbers to wear on the fronts and backs of their leotards during the audition class. Ellie's mom and Bethany's parents were given name badges to stick onto their clothes.

"This way, please," said Pamela, leading them to a studio with rows of seats. Ellie read the sign on the door. The Margot Fonteyn Studio. She gulped.

Many of the seats were already filled with parents and girls. The boys had their auditions on a different day.

"You two could be doing ballet class in here every day," said Bethany's dad, looking around the large room with its high ceiling and mirrored walls. "How about that?"

Ellie tried not to think about it. She was nervous enough already!

As they waited, more parents and girls came in, all looking around in awe. Ellie watched them enter and wondered which girls would make it through this audition. All of them wore their hair in buns or in the pinned-up braids worn for JAs, only without the ribbon bows. They had all been told to put a leotard on under their clothes, and most of them, like Ellie and Bethany, wore jeans and sweatshirts.

"Look, there's Grace!" said Bethany, waving as Grace and her parents took seats nearby.

"Isn't this scary?" whispered Grace. "There are so many people! Do you think they're all BADs?"

Just as she said this, a hush fell over the room and an elegantly dressed woman came in. "Good morning, everyone," she said brightly. "I'm Lynette Shelton, Director of The Royal Ballet School, and I'd like to welcome you all to the Lower School for the Final Audition."

Miss Shelton gave a short speech and explained how the audition schedule would work. She told the parents that they were welcome to have tea and coffee while they waited for their daughters. Then it was time to go!

A high-pitched chatter broke out in the room as girls started saying good-bye to their parents. Everyone was hugging and wishing one another good luck with pale, excited faces.

Ellie's mom hugged her tightly, and Ellie breathed in her mom's familiar perfume. "Just be yourself, honey," her mom told her. "You can do it. And *smile!*"

When the parents had gone, Pamela Dale and another lady divided the girls into two groups. To Ellie's relief, both Grace and Bethany were in her group. Ellie counted quickly—there were about twenty girls in each. That made forty girls at the Final Audition—more than she'd expected. There would only be places for ten or eleven girls, leaving the others devastated.

First, everyone went to a classroom, where they were asked to write about themselves. The teacher suggested they write about their family, their pets, or their likes and dislikes.

Ellie picked up her pen. She thought for a little while, and then began to write about moving from Chicago to Oxford. She wrote about her mom's job teaching art history at the university, and all the new friends they'd made. And she wrote about how she missed her grandparents and Heather. Before she knew it, they were asked to put down their pens.

Next Ellie's group had their ballet class. Ms. Dale took them to the changing room. A tall, pretty girl who looked about sixteen was waiting for them. "This is Nia," Pamela said. "She'll help you get ready."

Nia gave them a friendly smile. "Hello, everyone," she said. "I remember my own Final Audition, so I know you must be feeling pretty scared. I promise it won't be as bad as you think, though."

"It'll be worse," Bethany added in a low voice.

"No, it won't!" Nia called out. "It'll go so quick, it'll be over before you know it."

Bethany went bright red and giggled. "Whoops!" she said. "Did I say that out loud? My mouth is faster than my brain, sometimes!"

Everyone laughed, and Ellie felt the tension dissolve a little.

The girls all started getting undressed, whispering nervously to one another. Then Grace dropped her can of hair spray, and it crashed to the floor, making them all jump.

When the girls had finished helping one another attach their numbers to their leotards, they made their way back to the large studio. A feeling of disbelief came over Ellie. Reality check! Was she actually here, at White Lodge, in her leotard, about to dance?

The selection panel sat behind a long wooden table. There were six of them—four women and two men, all with notepads in front of them. They smiled as the girls filed in.

Miss Shelton stood beside a woman in ballet clothes at the front of the room. "This is Miss Carroll," she told the class. "She's going to teach your class this morning." Miss Shelton then introduced the selectors, who each nodded pleasantly to the class. Finally, she wished them luck and urged them to relax. "Just enjoy your dancing," she told them.

Miss Carroll arranged the girls along the barre in order of the numbers they were wearing, and then she introduced the pianist.

Ellie's heart was pounding so fast, she was convinced everyone else must be able to hear it. Then she thought of her mom. *You can do this, Ellie*, she reminded herself.

The class started with simple exercises, but Ellie could tell that everybody was trying their hardest. Each girl was holding her head just right, thinking about the position of her arms, turning her legs out from the hips, trying not to roll her feet or stick her rib cage out, holding her stomach, lengthening her back, lowering her shoulders.

After barre, just like at JAs, they had to do some steps in twos and threes. Miss Carroll kept mixing up the pairs, so that they danced with different people for each exercise. Ellie was really happy that she ended up with Grace for the waltz step—her favorite! Ellie just *knew* they looked good doing the exercise together.

Then Miss Carroll divided the group into two lines, one on either side of the studio, and showed them the step she wanted them to do. While they danced to swingy music, the lines had to cross each other diagonally.

"Left always goes in front of right—that's the rule of the stage," she told the girls.

Ellie did a quick head count and figured out that she had to pass behind number eighteen in the other line. The girl had red hair, and was easy to recognize.

The music began and the first girl in each line set off across the studio. Ellie kept her eye on the red-haired girl, but suddenly, the girl in front of Ellie passed behind the red-haired girl, in the place Ellie should have been!

Ellie panicked. She set off from her spot and crashed right into the red-haired girl, who gave Ellie a furious look! Ellie scrambled back into line and managed to make it to the corner, where she stood by the barre, feeling like a total klutz.

I've wrecked my chance, she thought in despair. *How could I have miscounted?*

Ellie counted the girls in the other line again. *Oh, no!* The red-haired girl must have swapped places with another girl when Ellie wasn't looking. *I should have double-checked!* Ellie thought miserably. *Now I've made a complete fool of myself!*

Somehow, she finished the class. Later, she couldn't even

remember what else they had done, or in what order, or when her legs finally stopped shaking. It all went by in a blur. By the time they did their *reverence*, Ellie's face was shiny and pink, and stray hairs were escaping from her bun in every direction.

As they left the studio, Ellie couldn't bring herself to look at anyone. She felt so embarrassed; she wished she were anywhere but here. She just wanted to be an ordinary kid again. *Whatever made me think I was good enough for The Royal Ballet School?* she asked herself.

"I feel awful," said Grace in the changing room.

Bethany, for the first time ever, said nothing at all.

"I guess we're all kind of drained after such a high," said a smiley girl, who introduced herself to everyone as Sophie.

"You probably all feel like collapsing," said Nia sympathetically, "so you'll be pleased to hear it's lunch now. After that, you'll have your interviews and physio assessments."

After lunch, Ellie's group was taken to a room in the old building, where everyone was assessed by the friendly school physiotherapist. He had to check each girl's heart, bone alignment, and overall physical health to make sure she was fit to dance.

The final part of the audition was an interview with the Head of the Lower School, Mr. Knott.

Mr. Knott's office was large, with tall windows. There were beautiful paintings on the walls and a huge wooden bookcase. Ellie sat on a chair facing Mr. Knott's desk.

"Well, Ellie, what do you like to do, apart from ballet?" Mr. Knott asked her.

Ellie's mind went blank. "I like swimming," she said finally. "And writing."

He made a note. "You enjoy English at school, then, I expect?" he said, smiling at her encouragingly.

"Yes," she stammered nervously. "And . . . uh . . . history. I liked learning about King Henry the Eighth and all his wives."

"I see you come from the United States," said Mr. Knott. "We have several overseas students here at the Lower School. Four, I believe, from America. Have you found life to be very different over here?"

Ellie nodded and started talking about basic things like using pounds instead of dollars, and how the cars were smaller, and then she found that she was talking about Oxford, and a torrent of words were coming out—about how amazing the buildings were, and how much she loved living in a city that had seen so much life and history, and how the shops were all so individual, like cottages, some of them, rather than the regular ones back in Chicago, and how Mom had taken her just the other day to one of the university libraries, and how it had even *smelled* old, and . . .

All of a sudden, Ellie was aware of just how much she was talking, and forced herself to stop, practically in the middle of a sentence. She'd messed up the dance class already. She didn't want to mess up the interview, too!

After a few more questions, Mr. Knott stood up, and Ellie

guessed it was the end of the interview. He had lots of other girls to see. He smiled and shook Ellie's hand, and she left his office.

She still felt glum at the thought of the dance class. How could she have been so stupid? Even though Grace said her mistake didn't matter, it did to Ellie. It mattered like nothing else had before!

When the interviews were done, Ms. Dale showed the girls around a very quiet, almost empty White Lodge. It was like being in a big house, not like a school at all.

"Where is everyone?" asked a girl standing near Ellie.

"Most of the students either go home or out shopping on Saturday afternoons," Ms. Dale explained. She opened the door to a bright, cheerful dorm room that was long and curved, in a crescent shape. There were posters on the walls, and the beds were covered with bright quilt covers and cushions. "This is the dormitory for girls in their first year," she said.

There was no one around, but as Ellie and the other hopefuls walked through the dormitory, they noticed messages scattered about the room. The Lower School students had left signed ballet shoes, or teddy bears, or cards with messages of good luck. Ellie felt Bethany nudge her in the ribs and looked up to see a banner that said: "Good Luck, Everyone Auditioning Today!"

"That was nice of them," said Grace.

It *was* nice, Ellie had to agree. But she was so sure she was never going to sleep in this room, she didn't even want to look at the messages. "Come on, we're getting left behind," she said, and pulled Grace away.

By now, it was late afternoon. It had been a long day, and Ellie wished she could just clamber into the car and take a nap. But Bethany's dad suggested that they all go out for dinner before driving home.

Ellie didn't eat much.

"You're quiet," her mom whispered. "Anything you want to talk about?"

Ellie picked at her food with her fork and shook her head. She kept picturing her mistake in class, over and over again.

"When do you think we'll hear whether we got in?" Bethany wondered.

"Soon, I would imagine," answered Mrs. Wilson.

"If they post the letters on Monday afternoon, they should arrive on Tuesday," Bethany's dad put in. "And before you say anything, Bethany, you *are* going to school on Tuesday morning, whether we've heard or not!"

When they got home, Ellie was so tired that she fell asleep on her bed with her clothes on. The next thing she knew, her mom was gently changing her into her pajamas. Ellie snuggled close to her mom. "I could sleep for a hundred years," she murmured.

"Sleeping Beauty?" suggested her mom.

"Very funny," Ellie said. "Mom, what if Bethany gets into the Lower School, and I don't?" The thought had been troubling her all the way home.

Ellie's mom took both Ellie's hands in hers. "Well, honey,"

she said softly, "you'll be disappointed, but you'll be happy for her, of course."

Her mom kissed her good night and turned out the light. Ellie lay in bed, thinking about what her mother had said. *Happy for Bethany?* She hoped so. Deep down, she knew there would be a horrible knot of jealousy, too.

Ellie sighed. She'd gone from being numb with tiredness to feeling wide awake, just thinking about the audition again. She switched on her lamp and pulled her diary out of her bag.

Dear Diary,

I'm so tired, but I can't sleep until I've written about today. It's hard to admit, but I just know that if Bethany gets a place at The Royal Ballet School and I don't, being happy for her will be a really, really big test for me. Maybe even bigger than the audition itself.

I don't even know what to think about the audition anymore. I have never felt so embarrassed as when I danced right smack into that girl in front of me! And I completely deserved the glare she gave me. But at least I didn't make any other big mistakes. I just have to hope that I did well enough to make them forget that one!

I feel like I could sleep for three days, so maybe I'll just do that—I can't imagine how else I'll get through all the hours between now and Tuesday morning. Please let me get in. PLEASE!!!

Ellie went to school as usual on Monday, although she found it almost impossible to concentrate. On Tuesday, Steve hadn't come with the mail by the time she and her mom had to leave for school and work. All day, Ellie imagined a white envelope sitting on the floor in the front hall, just waiting to be opened. It was absolutely unbearable.

"Ellie Brown, are you listening?" she heard Phoebe say as they sat at their lunch table. "Didn't you hear what I just told you? Mom said I could have a sleepover party this weekend!"

"Oh, sorry, Pheebs," Ellie said with a sigh. "I was thinking that if I took the bus home from school today, I might get home five minutes quicker than if I walked. I want to see if—"

"If your letter's arrived yet," Phoebe finished for her. "I know, I know. I do, too! I hope you realize you're turning me into a nervous wreck!"

Ellie laughed at her friend's comical expression. "Sorry," she said. "Let's talk about something else. Steve already promised he'd bring it over as soon as it arrives at the post office. Did I hear you say something about a sleepover?"

.   .   .   .

That evening, the doorbell chimed at the exact same moment as the phone rang. Ellie's mom grabbed the phone as Ellie called out, "I'll get the door."

It was Steve. Ellie's mom had invited him over for dinner. "Sorry, princess," he said when Ellie opened the door. "Nothing yet."

Ellie felt her shoulders slump. "Thanks anyway, Steve," she mumbled as they went into the kitchen.

Ellie's mom was on the phone, and she signaled to Ellie to come over. Ellie raised her eyebrows at her but couldn't guess who her mom was talking to. After a second or two, her mom said good-bye and handed the phone to Ellie, saying, "It's Mrs. Wilson."

Mrs. Wilson's voice was sad when Ellie said hi. "Bethany didn't get in," she said.

Ellie gasped. "Oh, no!" she said. "Poor Bethany!"

"She's too upset to talk to anyone right now," Mrs. Wilson went on, sounding pretty upset herself.

Ellie felt terrible. "Tell her I'm sorry," she said, with a lump in her throat. Poor, poor Bethany. "I'm so sorry. Is she going to Mrs. Franklin's tomorrow?"

"I hope so," said Mrs. Wilson. "She can't hide in her room forever. Anyway, Bethany just wanted you to know, Ellie. Your mum told me you haven't heard anything yourself yet. We'll keep our fingers crossed for you."

"Thanks," Ellie mumbled. She put the receiver down, feeling numb. Well, it was happening. Decisions had been made—and letters were being sent out. It was only a matter of time now before she knew if she'd been rejected, too.

·   ·   ·   ·

Bethany *did* show up at Mrs. Franklin's the next day. Ellie wasn't sure if she should hug her—she thought maybe it might make her cry—but Bethany came up and hugged her. "No letter yet?" she asked.

"Nope," Ellie replied.

"I've still got my fingers crossed for you," said Bethany with a weak smile.

"Thanks," Ellie said, grabbing her friend's hand and squeezing it tightly. She thought Bethany was really brave to come to ballet class and be so supportive of Ellie after her own huge disappointment. She watched Bethany sliding pins into her hair as usual. *Would I be able to do that?* Ellie wondered. *I'm not sure.*

Dear Diary,
　　These last two days have been awful. I've got dark circles under my eyes because I can't sleep. I probably flunked the English test yesterday—I was way too distracted to study.
　　Why can't the letter just come, and put me out of my misery? Where is it?

When Ellie got back from school on Friday afternoon to find there was *still* no letter, she felt like screaming. A whole week of waiting. It was like torture! And she knew that some of the letters had gone out—Bethany had had hers, obviously, and then, yesterday she'd had a breathless, practically hysterical call from Grace to say that she had got in!

So why hadn't Ellie heard? She just couldn't bear it. If she'd failed the audition, she wanted to know, so that she could start getting over it, like Bethany was doing.

Her mom came in and looked at her. "This is *awful*," she said. "I can't bear that anxious look on your face for another minute. And besides, *I'm* about to pass out with the suspense as well."

Ellie shrugged. "Steve would have brought the letter if it had come," she said. "What else can we do?"

Her mom picked up The Royal Ballet School's brochure with a determined look. "I'll tell you what we'll do," she said. "We'll phone them. Is that okay?"

Ellie's heart thumped painfully in her chest. "Now?" she asked.

"Right now," her mom said firmly.

Ellie took a deep breath. "Okay," she said. "Good idea."

Ellie waited beside her mom as she dialed, her heart beating fast.

"Hello," Ellie's mom said, when the phone was answered at the other end. "I'd like to speak to someone about the Final Audition results for the Lower School, please. Thank you." She put her hand over the receiver. "They're putting me through," she whispered.

Ellie put her head in her hands. Now that she was so close to finding out, she was starting to feel sick.

"Okay," her mom was saying. "Well, could she call me back, please? It's Amy Brown on Oxford 623197. Thanks very much."

She put the phone down. "The line was busy," she said. "Typical!"

Ellie groaned, and her mom put an arm around her. "Nearly there, sweetie," she said comfortingly. "We'll have something special for dinner—whether we're celebrating or making ourselves feel better—what do you say?"

"I know what you're going to suggest," Ellie said. "Fish-and-chips!"

She and her mom laughed, and then the phone rang and they both stopped abruptly. Then the doorbell rang.

"Why do those two always go at the same time?" her mom said. "I'll get the phone, you get the door," she added, grabbing the receiver. "Yes, this is Amy Brown," Ellie heard her say.

Ellie ran to the front door, and opened it to see Steve on the doorstep, holding up a white envelope. She stared at it in amazement. "What . . . ? Where . . . ?" she started to say.

Steve pressed it into her hand. "I've just found it wedged between a couple of big envelopes at the sorting office. I thought I'd bring it straight over, like I promised." He paused. "Well, aren't you going to open it, then?"

Ellie clutched the thick white envelope. Her hands felt shaky and sweaty, and her heart was pounding like crazy. She walked back toward the living room, where she could hear her mom still talking on the phone.

"I see," her mom was saying in a serious voice, and Ellie practically fell over. Oh, *no*. She obviously hadn't got in. Not if her mom sounded so solemn.

"Open it, Ellie!" Steve urged, his blue eyes excited.

"I understand," Ellie's mom went on. "Yes, Ellie told me about that."

Ellie felt as if her heart had frozen. They must be talking about when she had bumped into the girl with the red hair. It had ruined everything, Ellie knew it! And how awful, to find out this way—with Steve here, as well! She just knew she was going to cry, and she'd feel really embarrassed in front of him, and . . .

She ran to her bedroom. She had to do this in private. She'd open the letter and bawl her eyes out, where nobody could see her.

She shut her bedroom door and leaned against it, her heart hammering. Then she tore open the envelope and unfolded the letter.

"Dear Ellie," she read miserably, "I am very pleased to . . ."

Ellie blinked. Whoa . . . hold on. What was that?

"I am very pleased to offer you a place at The Royal Ballet School . . ."

Ellie gasped in disbelief. A place at The Royal Ballet School—did it really say that?

Yes, it did.

She'd done it! She'd gotten a place! She was going to The Royal Ballet School!

"I'm in!" she screamed, throwing the letter in the air and whirling around in shock and delight. "Yes!"

She ran back to the living room, just as her mom was hanging up the phone. Then they were a tangle of arms and kisses. "You did it!" her mom said tearfully, kissing Ellie's face and hair. "You did it, Ellie!"

Steve let out a whoop and came to hug both of them. Ellie's mom was crying and laughing at the same time. So was Ellie.

"But how come? I messed up so badly! What did they say?" Ellie gabbled, her eyes shining.

"They said that they were impressed by your passion and enthusiasm, Ellie," her mom told her. "They said they thought you were a natural . . ." She stroked Ellie's hair. "I guess that counts for more than your mistake."

"A natural," Ellie repeated, shaking her head in a daze. Then she laughed. "Wow!"

Ellie's mom was laughing, too. "I'm so proud of you, honey!" she said, hugging her again.

Dear Diary,

I'm still in shock—I can hardly believe it. I am going to the Lower School!

We called Grandma and Gramps right away, even though it was only seven in the morning there! Then I rushed next door to tell Pheebs. I started crying, and Phoebe hugged me, and then she started sniffling, too. "Oh, Ellie, I know this sounds selfish, but I AM going to miss you," she said. "We will still be friends, won't we? You will write to me and everything?"

"You bet I will," I said. "As if I'd lose a fantastic friend like you!"

After we'd stopped crying, Phoebe said that she really was pleased for me, and we made a promise that we would always be friends, no matter what, and that we would never miss each other's birthday parties. I'm gonna miss her like crazy, though.

When I told Bethany the news, she screamed so loud, I had to hold the phone away from my ear. She was soooo excited for me. You have to hand it to her—she's tough. I think that dancers must be some of the strongest people in the whole world.

Mom says Bethany will succeed in whatever she decides to do because she's got a big heart and an amazing attitude. She's right about that.

I'd better go and help Mom in the kitchen. She's cooking a celebration dinner— for us two, Steve, and the Mintons. I think I'll ask her if she wants to watch the Nutcracker video tonight before bed. Who knows, maybe one day, I really will dance the part of the Sugar Plum Fairy!

Royal Ballet School, HERE I COME!

GLOSSARY

ROYAL BALLET METHOD: An eight-year system of training and methodology developed and utilized by The Royal Ballet School to produce dancers with clean, pure classical technique

ARABESQUE: One leg is extended to the back (the name is taken from the flourished, curved line used in Arabic motifs)

BARRE: The horizontal wooden bar fastened to the walls of the ballet classroom or rehearsal hall that the dancer holds for support

BATTEMENT(S): To beat; a beating of the legs; see *grand battement* and *petit battement* for variations

BRAS BAS: The rounding of the arms held in front of the thighs with a small space between the hands

COUP DE PIED: Around the "neck" of the foot; one pointed foot is placed at the calf—just above the ankle—of the opposite leg

CROISÉ: To cross (in which the dancer faces the audience diagonally and has one leg crossed in front of the other)

DEMI-PLIÉ: A small bend (of the knees) in alignment over the toes, without causing the heel, or heels, of the foot to lift off the floor

DEVELOPPÉ: The unfolding of the working leg; the leg is drawn to the knee and then extended from there

ECHAPPÉ(S): To escape (a movement that begins in 5th position and moves quickly to 2nd position either by sliding feet to the ball of the foot or as a jump from 5th position to 2nd position)

FONDU(S): To melt (bending and extending of the legs at the same time with one leg supporting the body)

GRAND BATTEMENT: A throwing action of the fully extended leg in any direction with controlled lowering

GRAND PLIÉ: A deeper bend (of the knees) bringing the heels of the feet off the floor

PAS DE CHATS: Cat's step (because the movement is like a cat's leap); a jump where the legs are lifted and lowered separately, forming a diamond shape in the air

PETIT BATTEMENT: Small beat whereby a pointed foot "beats" in front and back of the calf—just above the ankle—of the opposite leg; this exercise is done with great rapidity

PIROUETTE: Turn (used to describe a turn, whirl, or spin); in the Russian method, they usually refer to turns as *tours*

PLIÉ(S): To bend (the knee or knees)

RELEVÉ(S): To rise (used to describe a rise from the whole foot to *demi-pointe* or full *pointe*)

RETIRÉ: Withdrawn (drawing up of the working foot to under the knee)

REVERENCE: A deep curtsey; performed at the end of class, as a mark of thanks and respect

SAUTÉS: To jump off the ground with both feet

TENDUS: Stretched; held-out; tight (in which a leg is extended straight out to the front *devant*, back *derrière*, or side *à la seconde*, with the foot fully pointed)